The Girl from Malta

Fergus Hume

The Girl from Malta

Copyright © 2024 Indo-European Publishing

The present edition is a reproduction of previous publication of this classic work. Minor typographical errors may have been corrected without note; however, for an authentic reading experience the spelling, punctuation, and capitalization have been retained from the original text.

ISBN: 979-8-88942-485-7

CONTENTS

CONTENTS

CHAPTER I

A RUINED LIFE

It was a calm southern night, with a silver moon shining serenely in a cloudless sky, and over the glittering expanse of ocean steamed the P. and O.'s vessel "Neptune" on her way from Brindisi to Malta. Every revolution of her powerful engines sent her plunging through the blue waters, with the waves breaking in tumbling masses of white foam from her towering sides. The passengers, numbering about three hundred, were all in high spirits, having had a most delightful voyage from Australia, and were looking forward, with pleasure, to their arrival at Valletta on the morrow.

Can there be anything in the world more pleasant than sea life on a steamship with jolly people? Anyone, who is a good sailor, will answer "No," though perhaps Ulysses, who travelled over these same waters, might not agree, but then the wandering Greek had not a P. and O. steamer at his command.

On this charming night a dance was in progress on the hurricane deck, and the immense area had been draped with brilliantly coloured flags, thus turning it into an admirable ball-room. Miss Kate Lester, the belle of the ship,—a position she knew she occupied, and, by the way took full advantage of all benefits to be derived therefrom,—was the pianist, and was playing the "Venetia Valse," to which a number of young people were dancing. The white dresses of the ladies, the darker costumes of the men, and the vivid tints of the flags, all seen under the powerful radiance of the electric lights, made up a very pretty picture.

Ronald Monteith thought so, at all events—and Mr. Monteith was a very good judge of beauty, especially if it were feminine. He leaned lazily against the bulwarks and surveyed the festive scene with a smile on his handsome face, but—Joseph like—took no notice of the many glances he received from bright eyes. Tall and sinewy, with fair hair and mustaches, blue eyes, and a skin bronzed by exposure to the hot southern sun, Monteith was decidedly good-looking, and by no means undervalued his personal appearance. His father was a wealthy Australian squatter, who owned large stations in the Riverina District, and, being a liberal-minded and liberal-handed man, had sent his son forth to see the world. Master Ronald, nothing loth, departed with a goodly supply of money, several

1

letters of introduction, and a huge capacity of enjoyment; so, as can easily be seen, this lucky young man's lines were cast in pleasant places. There were lots of pretty girls on board who would have liked to marry him, nevertheless, his highness threw his handkerchief to none of them, yet flirted with all. He was not a clever man by any means, but he could ride, shoot, swim and box to perfection, all of which athletic accomplishments found favour in the eyes of women; he was, moreover, an honourable gentleman, with a kind heart and a generous spirit.

As he stood there in a meditative attitude, wondering if he could summon up sufficient courage to dance with the thermometer at somewhere about eighty, a young fellow who rejoiced in the name of Patrick Ryan, came up and took him by the arm.

"Come and have a drink, me boy," said Mr. Ryan, with a slight touch of the brogue. "I'm half dead with dancin', not to mention the way I've to talk to the girls, and tell 'em enough lies to make me recordin' angel take to shorthand."

"Then why the deuce don't you stop it?" retorted Ronald, as he accepted this bacchanalian invitation, and they went down to the bar.

"Oh, begad, think how the girls would tear their hair, and mine too, if I didn't look after them," replied Pat; "it's purely ornamental ye are, but 'tis better to be good than beautiful, and a mighty poor consolation anyhow."

Pat Ryan was certainly not beautiful, being short and dark, but his lack of good looks was more than made up by the possession of a clever tongue, which was generally going from morning till night, and as he could sing, play, write verses, and flatter a woman to perfection he was a great favourite on board.

"Well, I'm off to the halls of dazzlin' light," he observed when they had finished their drinks and were once more on deck; "come along, ye lazy divil, and I'll get you a partner."

"I'm too hot," objected Ronald, putting his hands in his pockets.

"Oh, jist hear him," said Pat in disgust. "Why, I've seen ye all day in the saddle under a burnin' sun, and divil a growl from ye, and yet when I offer ye a pretty girl to dance with, ye refuse; and as for the girl, begad, her beauty would tempt St. Anthony himself and small blame to him."

"Who is she?" asked the Australian, with some show of interest.

"Miss Lester, no less."

"I thought you were sweet there yourself Pat."

"I'm sweet on all the girls me boy—there's safety in numbers, and I believe in quantity as well as quality."

2

"You're getting too deep for me," said Ronald, pulling a very black pipe from his pocket, "so I'll go and have a smoke."

"A pipe too!" echoed Pat; "faith, it's woman's greatest enemy."

"And man's greatest friend," retorted Monteith, as he strolled off.

Pat, laughing, went away to arrange another dance, and to this end asked Mrs. Pellypop to play the Lancers. Mrs. Pellypop, tall, majestic and aggressively virtuous, was the mother-in-law of a Bishop, and was on her way home to pay her daughter a visit, an event regarded by the worthy prelate with anything but unmixed joy. She had an eye-glass—very effective to crush presuming people—a chilling smile and very strong opinions about her own position; in short she was a type of all that was virtuous and—disagreeable.

While the dancing was thus going on Ronald, having lighted his pipe, strolled up and down the long deck for a few minutes, then leaned meditatively over the side and watched the glittering waters sweeping past. While thus engaged he felt a light touch on his arm, and, on turning round, saw a man he knew standing near him.

"Hullo, Ventin," said Ronald, removing his beloved pipe for a moment, "why aren't you dancing?"

"Because I hate dancing," retorted Mr. Ventin irritably; "I'm sick of the perpetual jangle of that d—d piano, of Miss Lester's flirtations, and of Mother Pellypop's virtues—I'm sick of the whole thing and I wish the voyage were over."

"I don't," replied Ronald taking a seat on one of the deck chairs; "it's very jolly I think."

"Yes, I daresay," said Ventin gloomily; "you are young and rich, with all the world before you. I, on the contrary, am old."

"Rubbish!"

"If not in years, at least in experience. I have lost all my illusions, and have discovered the gold of fancy to be only the tinsel of reality. You stand on the threshold of a happy career; I can only look back on a ruined life."

Ronald looked at him curiously as he spoke. A handsome face certainly, but with innumerable wrinkles and hollow cheeks; dark, piercing, restless eyes; black, smooth hair touched with white at the temples; and a thin-lipped mouth, with a heavy, dark mustache. Yes, Lionel Ventin was handsome, but one whom a woman would rather fear than admire. For the rest, a slender figure, high-bred manner, and in general a cool, nonchalant demeanour, which but ill accorded with the restless glances of his eyes on this particular night.

Ronald had been introduced to him in Melbourne a year

3

previously, and then lost sight of him, never expecting to set eyes on him again. But the first person he met on board the "Neptune" was Ventin, and a strong friendship soon sprung up between them, which seemed quite unaccountable, considering the difference in their dispositions. But the fact was Ventin liked Ronald's happy, pleasant manner, and, on his part, Monteith felt for the other that strong admiration which a young man always has for one who is older and knows more about the world than himself. Ventin had been everywhere, and seen everything. He had shot big game in the Rocky Mountains, hunted elephants in Africa and tigers in India, knew London, Paris, and Vienna thoroughly, and, when he chose to exert himself, could be a most delightful companion. To-night however, he seemed restless and ill at ease, which rather surprised Ronald accustomed, as he was, to the cool, careless manner of his friend.

"I don't know why the deuce I should trust you," said Ventin, sitting down near Ronald and eyeing him keenly; "we are only fellow-travellers, and I am not usually given to confidences, but occasionally it does a man good to open his heart to someone."

"Fire away old boy," said Ronald, puffing out a big cloud of smoke, and settling himself comfortably in his chair; "you look like a man with a history."

"Happy the nation that has no history," quoted Ventin, cynically. "I suppose the same remark applies to a man's life. My history begins in that accursed Malta, for it was there I met her."

"Oh! a woman?"

"Of course; most men's histories commence and end with a woman, that is why confidences are so monotonous. Well," turning restlessly in his seat, "I may as well say Ventin is not my real name. No—it is—well I need not tell you my real name, as it is quite unnecessary. I didn't do much credit to it when I had it, and I daresay my present name is not quite blameless. Bah! Why do I sentimentalize? Forty years of life ought to have knocked all that out of me."

"You're not forty!" said Ronald looking curiously at him.

"Why?" asked Ventin quickly turning his haggard face towards the Australian; "do you think these wrinkles due to age or dissipation?—To both I'm afraid, though I suspect the latter has had more to do with them than the former. God made man in His own image. He can't be very delighted when He sees how hard we strive to mar His handiwork."

There was silence for a few minutes, and the two men could hear the regular beating of the screw, the fitful sound of music mellowed by distance, and the gay laughter of the dancers. The

4

voices of the whist players, disputing over some point in their game, came from the smoking-room, and in the semi-darkness extending along the deck could be heard the soft notes of a woman's voice, or the deeper tones from a man.

Then Ventin began to speak in slow, measured tones, quite different from his former vehement style.

"I was never a good young man," he said cynically; "but I don't think I was worse than the generality of fellows. Give a boy money and place him amid the temptations of London, and, in nine cases out of ten, he'll go to the devil, or, if he doesn't go, it is because some lucky accident prevents him. Perhaps he has a man-of-the-world friend who advises him—or he loses his money, and has to leave the primrose path—or, he may marry a good woman, and her influence may save him from his worst enemy, himself. Ah! if we only knew the value of a good woman's love—how she can be our guardian angel, and keep us pure and honourable in the midst of temptation! But we never find out the value of such treasures till it's too late,—but there,"—with a weary sigh,—"I am sentimentalizing again! Let me go on with my story.

"I lost both parents at the age of twenty, and I went to London with plenty of money and no experience whatever. Unluckily, I had no one to play the part of Mentor to my Telemachus, so I had to gain wisdom by experience, and pretty dearly I paid for it. I became a hard, cynical man of the world, for a thirteen years' residence in London was a liberal education to me in the nil admirari philosophy of to-day, and then—well my money lasted longer than my health, and I became seriously ill—so bad indeed that my doctors ordered me to Malta to be cured. Oh, heavens how ironical is Fate—it was merely a case of out of the frying-pan into the fire—for my part I prefer the frying-pan. It was true the balmy air and bright skies of Malta cured me of one disease, but unfortunately I contracted another not so easily dealt with,—that of love.

"I became acquainted with two charmingly pretty girls of the ages of twenty-three and nineteen, and—forgive my apparent egotism—both fell in love with me. It was the choice of Hercules over again, but unluckily I chose the wrong lady, and married the elder. 'Hell has no fury like a woman scorned,' so the younger soon hated me like poison, and left Malta for England. I married the woman of my choice and then my punishment commenced. She was a perfect devil, with nothing but her beauty to recommend her. Her father boasted they had Arab blood in their veins, and my belief is that the ancestor of the family must have been Eblis himself. Often and often she threatened to kill me for some petty thing, and I believe she would had not some instinct of danger restrained her. If

5

I looked at another woman, there was a storm of reproaches—if I were away for a day, her jealous mind conjured up a hundred infidelities—in short, our married life was a hell upon earth. At last, after a year of this cat-and-dog existence, I determined to leave her, and to this course she assented, after a good deal of persuasion. A deed of separation was drawn up, by which I allowed her a handsome income on condition that she resided in Valletta. She agreed to this and, after a stormy parting, I went to England, and lived there a moody, discontented man."

"You did not see the other sister?" asked Ronald.

"No," he replied; "I never set eyes on her again. She was a nice girl, and I dare say I did treat her badly by leading her to believe I cared for her.

"Well, I wandered all over the United Kingdom and, while staying with some friends in the Highlands, I met the woman who made a better man of me—for a time. She was an orphan was Elsie Macgregor. Her father had been a soldier who died of consumption contracted in the trenches of Sebastopol, during the Crimean War. Fair and slender, with quiet, blue eyes and hair like yellow corn—I loved her devotedly—yes, too well to wrong her innocence, and would have gone away in silence, but she, with a woman's keen instinct, saw there was something wrong, and begged me to tell her all. I did so, and she—oh, Monteith, what do you think she did?—left her home and her friends—defied the sneers of the world and the scornful looks of her own sex and became my mistress. Yes—she saw that hers alone was the hand that could arrest me in my downward course; so to save me she ruined herself. I lived with her for one happy year, and always looked back to that time as the brightest era in my life.

"Then my devil of a wife found me out and instituted proceedings in the Divorce Court against me. I did not object, as I thought I would then be free to marry Elsie. The decree was pronounced, and as soon as I was able I married Elsie and took my passage with her to Australia—there intending to start a new life in a new land. We built castles in the air of a happy future, but it was not to be; for, just as the ship was leaving, that Maltese devil came on board, and then a fearful scene took place. I cannot describe to you the terrible way she went on, and Elsie, being in delicate health, clung to my arm nearly fainting. At last the climax came, for my former wife sprang forward and struck Elsie on the face—the poor girl fell in a faint on the deck, and after considerable difficulty that Maltese fiend was removed by force from the ship. We sailed, and I thought Elsie would soon recover, but the iron had entered into her soul, and before we rounded the Cape she was buried at sea."

6

Here Ventin covered his face with his hands, and Ronald, respecting his emotion, said nothing.

After a few moments of silence, Ventin resumed in an unsteady voice:

"I landed in Australia, a broken-hearted man—heedless of my life, and with no hope of happiness in the future. I went from Australia to New Zealand, thence to America, and travelled all over the new world trying to drown my bitter thoughts in dissipation, but without success. I went in for gambling, drinking, racing, threw away money on women, kept a theatre; in fact did everything I could to ruin myself. Then, wearied of the reckless life I was leading, I went back to Australia and tried to settle down, but it was no use. Like Orestes, pursued by the Furies, I had to fly, so I took my passage on board the 'Neptune,' and thus, here you find me a ruined cynic at the age of forty, and all through a woman."

"And what do you intend to do when you reach England?" asked Ronald, who had been listening with the deepest interest.

"England!" murmured Ventin dreamily; "perhaps I may never see England."

"What do you mean?" asked the Australian, a little startled as the thought of suicide flashed across his mind.

"No not that," replied Ventin, guessing his thoughts, "but when I was in Australia I received a letter from my first wife saying she would kill me the first time we met."

"She would never dare——"

"Oh yes she would—she has Arab blood in her veins remember; and when she is mad with rage, she would put a knife in me and take the consequences."

"But are you sure the letter was from her?"

"Who else could it be from?" said Ventin, shrugging his shoulders; "it was not signed, and the handwriting was slightly different from her usual style, but then she often threatened to kill me, and I've no doubt puts into writing what she often said."

"You have no enemies?"

"None that would go so far as to desire my death. No my friend, the letter was from the charming Maltese, and she'll carry out her purpose if she can."

"Is she in Valletta?"

"I don't know; if she is, and find me out, well—I may reach England alive, but I doubt it; and after all I don't think I'd care much: I'm sick of life, and if one could be only certain that death is an eternal sleep—well," with a sneer, "I think I'd be inclined for the nap; but come," rising to his feet, "I've bored you enough for one

7

night, let us go into the smoking-room and have one pipe before turning in."

Ronald assented, and walked slowly after Ventin, wondering at the strange story he had heard, and at the strange man who told it to him.

"He's had a queer life," mused Monteith as they stepped into the smoking-room. "I wonder if his end will be as queer."

The dance being over all the ladies had gone below, the electric lights were out in the saloon and on deck, and only the smoking-room was lighted up for the benefit of the night-birds. Here they all came flushed and excited with their exercise, and soon all the marble-topped tables were covered with glasses containing different beverages from whisky-and-soda down to a modest squash, while the atmosphere resembled nothing so much as a London fog. Ventin had recovered his spirits, and told stories, made epigrams, and sang songs, until Ronald could hardly believe he saw before him the same man who had told him such a pitiful story.

Ventin saw his friend's eyes directed curiously at him once or twice, and guessing the meaning of his looks, came up to him to say "Good-night."

"I've put on the cap and bells, you see," he said, cynically; "broken hearts are not in favour with the world, and life is only a masquerade after all."

CHAPTER II

IN THE STRADA REALE

Tunisians, Maltese, English, Italians! Was there ever such a motley crowd as that collected in the principal street of Valletta? Bare-kneed Highlanders, in their picturesque tartans, elbowed wide-trousered Mahomedans from Tunis and Fez; swarthy, black-eyed Italians from Naples jostled against red-coated Tommy Atkins as he swaggered along, and the ascetic face of a priest, looking severely from under his long shovel hat, was seen close to the piquant countenance of a Maltese damsel, blushing under her ugly, black silk hood as she tripped gaily onward attended by her watchful duenna. Here and there parties of tourists came laughing and joking along the crowded pavement. English ladies, lithe and bright-looking in their neat-fitting yachting costumes, accompanied by smart young gentlemen, who had left their clubs and offices for a breath of the invigorating Mediterranean air, and crowds of ragged beggars were shrieking for money, and never satisfied with what they got. Such a mass of colour, such a diversity of costumes, such a confusion of tongues, and over all the clear blue sky, with the hot sun blazing down on the tall white houses and steep narrow streets.

The "Neptune" cast anchor about two o'clock in the afternoon and, according to the notice posted at the top of the saloon stairs, would not leave till nine o'clock at night, so all the passengers—the men in flannels and straw hats and the ladies in white dresses with sunshades—went on shore to enjoy themselves. The great ship steamed majestically into the still, blue waters of the Grand Harbour, and cast anchor under the massive walls which rose in towering heights from the precipitous rocks, and still bore on their weather-beaten fronts, which had withstood so many rude assaults, the proud crests of the famous Order of St. John of Jerusalem. On each side stood the cities of Valletta and The Borgo with their square, flat-roofed houses showing white and clear as they arose in serrated masses against the vivid, blue sky, and all round the big steamer innumerable boats, with canopies erected in the stern to keep off the sun, were darting about impelled by screaming, vociferating boatmen who had more conversation than clothes. Down the side of the ship the passengers went in a never-ending stream, and as boat after boat was filled with a laughing crowd and sheered off, there was soon quite a procession to the shore. It appeared as if the ship would be quite empty, save for the crew; but one, at least of the passengers, remained behind. This was Lionel Ventin, who preferred a lazy day on board with a pipe and novel to the discomfort of exploring the steep streets and picturesque buildings of Valletta.

"I'm sick of Malta," he said, in reply to Ronald's persuasions; "I know every hole and corner of that confounded Valletta, and agree with Byron about it; besides," with a significant glance, "I might meet my wife."

Against this last argument Ronald had nothing to urge, so went down to join his party, which consisted of Mrs. Pellypop, tall and majestic, in black silk, Kate Lester, and the irrepressible Pat Ryan. As they moved off, Ventin, who was arrayed in a suit of spotless white, waved his straw hat to them.

"How sulky that Mr. Ventin is," said Miss Lester, as they were pulled rapidly towards the shore; "he never speaks to anyone.

"Shows his bad taste," replied Mr. Ryan, "considerin' the pretty girls on board."

Mrs. Pellypop froze him.

"Your remark is flippant," she rejoined, putting up her glasses.

"It's true for all that," answered Pat bravely; "and ye'll see how these foreign chaps will stare at ye to-day, mam."

No woman is too old for flattery, and though Mrs. Pellypop was rigorously virtuous she was also a woman, so she received Pat's compliment very graciously.

"I know all about Valletta," she began. "I——"

"The deuce ye do," murmured Pat, "ye must know some nice things anyhow."

"And," continued she "will be your guide."

The other three looked at one another in dismay, and, with a strong effort, Pat gasped out a word of thanks.

"I say," whispered Ronald to Miss Lester, "she'll be as bad as Murray's guide book."

"Yes but not so accurate!"

"Never mind," said Pat, in a low tone, answering the last remark; "she'll make up for her mistakes by her obstinacy in stickin' to 'em; and perhaps," consolingly, "if we've luck we'll lose her."

They arrived on the rocky shore of Mount Sceberras, whereon Valletta stands, and admired the massive walls and the broad gateway, at which several red-coated sentries were keeping guard. Numerous guides offered their services but Mrs. Pellypop, in the purest of English—of which they did not understand one word, though her gestures were eloquent enough—sent them all away, and marched into Valletta, at the head of her party of three, like a victorious general into a conquered city. Then they began to climb the steep street leading to the Strada Reale, and under a burning sun the exercise was not pleasant. Oh! those interminable steps, how many oaths have they not been answerable for since Lord Byron abused them so heartily! Both Pat and Ronald cursed under their breaths, and if Miss Lester had not been very strictly brought up she also might have been tempted to use a word beginning with "D." Mrs. Pellypop, however, clad in her black silk—which must have been awfully hot, but extorted no remark from that excellent woman—toiled steadily upward, and not a word did this indomitable female say, though, like the celebrated parrot, she no doubt thought a lot.

"Capital exercise isn't it," observed Miss Lester as they paused for breath.

"I dare say, if we were training for a circus," retorted Pat dryly, taking off his straw hat. "I'm like Arethusa, and will melt into a stream of water if this goes on. I believe old Pellypop will swear shortly."

Kate laughed and looked at Mrs. Pellypop who, unassisted, was climbing slowly up the endless stairs.

"I don't think you gentlemen are very gallant," observed Kate, demurely glancing at Pat and Ronald walking on either side of her, "or you'd offer to help the old lady."

"We prefer to help the young lady," they cried in chorus, and Miss Lester blushed, not ill-pleased at this tribute to her charms.

On reaching the Strada Reale they found the place already crowded with their fellow-passengers, and after a few recognitions and salutations, Mrs. Pellypop's party went into one of the shops, where the ladies bought lace and the young men cigarettes. Ronald also purchased some lace handkerchiefs in order to pay off certain debts incurred by playing phillipine after dinner with sundry ladies on board, and, judging from the cost of his forfeits, he must have found the game somewhat expensive.

The next thing to be done was to see the celebrated Church of St. John, the glory of Valletta, so thither they went, and beheld a depressing-looking building not by any means remarkable for architectural beauty. But they were amply repaid for their disappointment by the magnificent sight which met their eyes on stepping out of the hot sunlight into the semi-gloom of the great building.

The arched roof covered with paintings of scenes from the life of St. John the Baptist, the exquisite tapestries hanging low down on either side, the vividly tesselated pavement under which so many valiant knights lay buried, and, to crown all, the wonderful

11

appearance of the grand altar, glittering with gold—all this made up a marvellous picture, which for brilliancy of colour and harmony of effect, has not its equal in the world.

After admiring the splendour of the central nave for some time, they went into all the side chapels—each of which was dedicated to a special language—and saw the tombs of dead and gone Grand Masters, and also the famous silver gates, one of the few things on the island that Napoleon did not carry away.

"Fancy how grand and inspiring it must have been," observed Mrs. Pellypop seizing the occasion to moralize, as befitted the mother-in-law of a Bishop. "When this place was thronged by noble knights, all in the different dresses of their orders, when——"

"Yes, rather jolly being a knight," interrupted Ronald, "shouldn't mind it myself."

"I should," said Pat, flippantly; "they weren't allowed to marry, and what is home without a mother?"

Miss Lester laughed, but Mrs. Pellypop was so disgusted by the giddy way in which the young man spoke, that she hastily left the church, having first reflected however, that there was nothing more to be seen.

"That young man would joke at his father's funeral," she said to Kate when they were once more in the hot sunshine.

"Well there's nothing like making the best of things," retorted Pat, who was just behind and overheard the remark.

"But really the church was grand," cried Ronald quickly in order to prevent a storm.

"Lots of show and very little religion I fancy," said the irrepressible Pat.

"I don't agree with you Mr. Ryan," observed Mrs. Pellypop, severely; "the solemn grandeur of that church would have an effect even on the most frivolous mind," with a significant glance at the Irishman.

"I daresay the effect wouldn't endure long," said Ronald, lightly. "Religion, which appeals purely to the senses, is never so strong as that which comes straight to the mind."

"Of course not," replied Pat who knew nothing about what he was talking, and only spoke to irritate the old lady, "I'd back Presbyterianism against Catholicism any day for fanaticism: it's a fight between Calvin and Peter—two to one on the winner."

Mrs. Pellypop made no reply, being struck with horror at the light way in which the young man treated religion, and walked hastily away with Miss Lester so as to close the discussion.

"Hang it Pat!" said Ronald, as they walked slowly behind, "why can't you leave the old girl alone?"

"Because she won't leave us alone," retorted Pat. "Why the deuce should she come with us to spoil sport?"

"Two young men and only one girl isn't sport!"

"Oh begad! we'd have tossed for her, and the loser could have made himself scarce."

They then went to the Capuchin Convent and saw the dried monks, looking grim and ghastly enough in the dim light of candles carried by their living brethren. Pat's comment on their appearance was original.

"They look like Bombay duck," he said, alluding to the dried fish usually eaten with curry. "I don't think I'll touch any more of it."

Kate Lester laughed.

"You are amusing, but irreligious," she said, turning away.

"Irreligious, certainly," observed Virtue, in the person of Mrs. Pellypop; "but amusing, no."

"I don't think the old thing's got much sense of humour," whispered Pat to Ronald as they went up again into the light of day.

"Well, if no one else laughs at your jokes, Pat, you always do yourself," retorted the Australian consolingly. "But come along, we'll go to the Barraca and see the view."

They strolled slowly along, inhaling the fresh air, and going through the ruined Barraca, which was unroofed by one of the Grand Masters, they stepped out on to the terrace, and saw that wonderful panorama, which is one of the finest things in Valletta. A magnificent view of the open sea, the blue waters of the Quarantine Harbour, while immediately below are the Sultan's garden, the huge walls of Fort Lascaris, and the Fish Market. Away in the distance can be seen Fort Sant Elmo protecting the entrance to the port, Fort St. Angelo, which is one of the oldest in Malta, and the angular lines of fortification standing sharp and clear against the vividly blue sky. It was a gorgeous panorama, and even Mrs. Pellypop was impressed.

"This place is impregnable," she said, surveying it through her glasses.

"I don't think so," said Pat, in a contradictory tone; "a few of our new guns would knock it to pieces in no time."

Mrs. Pellypop deigned no reply to this flippant remark, but walked off indignantly, wishing that the fate he intended for Valletta would befall this intrusive young man.

Suddenly Ronald uttered an exclamation:—

"By Jove! what pretty girls!"

Valletta, its traditions, its views, its pleasures, all vanished to nothing as he saw before him feminine beauty. Mrs. Pellypop was disgusted, as she considered no man had a right to admire a woman

13

when another was beside him. This however was merely the Pellypop code, and not generally adopted.

But the two ladies who had caused Ronald's exclamation fully justified his remark. One was tall and slender, with a dark, oval face, and coils of jet-black hair wreathed round her small head. Wonderfully dark eyes which had a sleepy look, a straight, delicately chiselled nose, and a full red mouth. She was dressed in a loose, white gown, with a crimson sash round her waist, and instead of the ugly hoods generally worn by the Maltese ladies, had a saucy sailor hat on her head, long Suède gloves, and a tall pompadour umbrella of red silk, completed her costume.

The other was somewhat similar in appearance, but evidently older, and had rather a repelling expression of countenance. She was dressed in black, and did not show to such advantage as her companion, so, after a careless glance at her, Ronald—who, like all fair men, admired dark women—turned his attention to the younger of the two. They appeared to have been quarrelling, and the younger girl was walking quickly a little in advance of her friend with an indignant expression on her face, while the other followed more slowly with a frown on her strongly marked features. When they disappeared, Ronald turned to his companion with a sigh.

"Yes awfully pretty."

"I confess," observed Mrs. Pellypop, slowly, "I do not think so."

Ronald was discreet, and surrendered.

"I dare say not," he observed hastily, "but you see one is so often deceived by a passing glance."

They wandered all over the city—went to the market and bought fruit, and were warned against eating it by an officious Maltese—saw the Armoury in the Grand Master's Palace—strolled round St. George's Square, and viewed with patriotic pride the flattering inscription to British Power over the Main Guard-House—sat in the carriage of the last Grand Master, and then went and had a light afternoon meal at a well-known hotel. It was now getting late, so, with a farewell glance at the Strada Reale and its queer crowd, they went down to the water-gate, where they found their boat waiting. A crowd of passengers was there, full of excitement about bargains made and experiences gained, and some guilelessly thought they had got the better of the Maltese shopmen, a thing quite impossible in this enlightened age.

They rowed to the steamer through the dark waters, with the lights of the city gleaming like stars in the distance, and the tall forms of ships looming like phantoms in the gloom. At last, after an adventurous journey, they arrived on board, and the first thing Ronald saw was Ventin leaning over the bulwarks watching fresh

14

arrivals. As soon as Mrs. Pellypop and Kate, escorted by Pat, had gone below, Ronald went to Ventin.

"Have you been on board all day?" he asked.

Ventin shook his head.

"No; I changed my mind and went on shore shortly after you left."

"Did you see her?"

"I did."

"The devil—did she see you?"

"I think so."

"Oh, so she didn't speak to you?"

"No! I was afraid of a scene, and came back to the ship at once."

"Well, she won't come on board now," said Ronald, consolingly; "so you'll be all right."

Ventin sighed.

"Nothing is so certain as the unforeseen," he replied, mournfully.

CHAPTER III

FOUND DEAD

The excitement of arrival at a new place is only equalled by the excitement of departure, and as the "Neptune" was to leave at nine o'clock no one thought of going to bed until the anchor was up.

The deck was crowded with passengers talking gaily about their adventures during the day, and here and there could be seen the strange faces of new arrivals on board. All round the steamer numerous boats, each bearing a light, were cruising about, and the water looked as if covered with restless fire-flies. Every now and then the whistle would sound in order to summon heedless passengers who had forgotten the hour of sailing. A lot of people had come to see new passengers off, and some were having a parting glass at the bar, while others were talking together in knots on deck. It was a very animated scene, and Ronald, standing by Ventin, felt amused at the chatter and bustle that was going on. Ventin however, eyed the crowd in his usual gloomy manner, and Ronald could not help asking him the cause of his lowering looks.

"Nothing more than common," he answered, carelessly; "I've seen all this sort of thing so often, it has become dreary—I'm bored, and I detest being bored."

"Are you afraid of seeing your wife?"

"Well, I don't know," replied Ventin, pulling his mustache; "if she thinks she can make a row she certainly will, but as I am under another name she will ask for me by my real one, and therefore she will be told there's no such person on board."

"And then?" interrogatively.

"Oh as she saw me in Valletta to-day she will think I'm stopping there, and hunt everywhere for me—I hope her patience will be rewarded—by the way, when do we start?"

"Nine o'clock," replied Ronald, looking at his watch, "it's now half-past eight."

"I'll go to bed, I think," observed Mr. Ventin, holding out his hand.

"Won't you wait till we start?"

"Too sleepy," yawned the other.

"Well if your fellow-traveller enters later you will be awakened."

"I daresay," said Ventin; "but I've got a whole cabin to myself—queer you haven't seen some things you'd like to look at."

16

"What is the number?" asked Monteith, carelessly.

"Forty-three."

Some one pushed against Ronald at that moment and he did not hear Ventin's answer.

"What number did you say?"

"Forty-three," from Ventin, in a louder tone of voice, "look me up in the morning—at present, good-bye," and he shook the young man's hand cordially.

"Good night you mean," said Ronald, laughing.

"It's all the same thing," replied Ventin, idly, "like Kathleen Mavourneen—it may be for years and it may be for ever—good night," and he moved away slowly down the saloon steps.

Ronald remained leaning over the bulwarks looking at the stream of people coming up, and presently he was joined by Pat Ryan, who made facetious remarks on the late arrivals.

"How much sham jewellery have ye got, Chester?" he asked of a fair young man who came lurching up, evidently having more on board than he could carry. Mr. Chester made some unintelligible reply, and Pat resumed, "Oh! it's sham-pagne ye took instead; it's a bad pun, but a heavenly truth. That you Bentley: how many girls have you mashed to-day? Begad, if your success has only been equal to your knowledge of Maltese it's mighty small progress ye've made. Ah! Monteith me boy, that's a pretty girl in black, I hope she's come on board to stop; keep your wicked eyes off her, ye villain, or I'll set Mrs. Pellypop on to you."

The girl in question was neither pretty nor fascinating, but Pat's tongue, once started, never knew when to stop; and Ronald was just going to march him off to the bar as the only way of closing his mouth, when the last bell was rung, and the cry of "All aboard for the shore" was heard.

A rush took place to the side, and a black line of people streamed down the gangway, then the ladder was lifted up; the old and new passengers lined the bulwarks and sang out "good-byes" to their friends in the darkness—the anchor was tripped—the whistle blew, and the throb of the engines announced that the "Neptune" was once more on her way to England.

"I wonder if anyone is left behind," said Ronald to Ryan, as they went to the smoking-room.

"They must be deaf if they are," retorted Pat; "that divil of a whistle would wake the dead—now me boy, what is it to be?"

"Whiskey and soda for me," said Monteith, when they were comfortably established in the smoking-room, through the wide doorway of which they could see the lights of Valletta fading slowly away.

17

"I'll follow suit," said Pat promptly, lighting his pipe. "Two whiskeys and soda, steward, and not too much soda."

All the ladies, tired with their experiences of Valletta, had gone to bed, and the smoking-room was filled with gentlemen whose tastings of the wines of the country had made them more exhilarated than usual. Being convivially disposed they ordered more liquor, and prepared to make a night of it.

"Where's Ventin?" asked Pat.

"Gone to bed," replied Monteith, knocking the ashes from his pipe.

"The deuce he has," said Ryan with surprise; "that's unusual for him."

"Tired I suppose," was the answer.

"It's a pity," observed Ryan, regretfully; "he is a deuced good fellow for a song."

"Give us one yourself Pat," said Bentley, tapping his glass on the table.

"Mr. Ryan for a song gentlemen."

"Yes a song—a song"—from all.

"Something jolly?" from Chester, who was now quite intoxicated.

"I'll sing ye 'Killaloe,'" said Pat; "it's got a touch of the brogue about it that will go beautifully with the whiskey."

So he accordingly sang "Killaloe" to a delighted audience, who joined in the chorus with bacchanalian vehemence, and who gave the "Whoop ye divils" at the end with a vigour worthy of Donnybrook Fair. Then Ronald sang, "Wrap me up in my old stable jacket"—that old song which is always such a favourite; and after sundry other selections had been given by gentlemen with good intentions, but husky voices, Pat was called on to sing his favourite nigger song, "I love a lubly gal." A pleasant voice had Pat, and he sang the plaintive little melody in a charmingly sympathetic manner—

> "I love a lubly gal, I do,
> And I have loved a gal or two;
> An' I know how a gal should be
> Lub'd—you bet I do."

Ronald found himself humming it as he went to bed, and then fell to sleep, and dreamt the dark girl he had seen that day in Valletta was the "lubly gal" he loved.

* * * * *

18

Next morning they were out of sight of land, afloat on the blue waters, with the blue sky above them. Ronald was up early, as he found it too hot to remain below, and having had his tub and arrayed himself in his flannels, he went on deck to have a smoke before the ladies put in an appearance. The lascars were washing down the deck, and disturbing numerous sleepers who had been taking their rest all night upstairs for the sake of coolness. One of these was Pat, who came stumbling out of the smoking-room in his pyjama, with a fur rug under one arm and a pillow under the other.

"Hullo Pat," said Monteith, laughing; "you look as if you were going to the pawnbroker."

"I want to go to bed," retorted Pat crossly; "those divils in the smoking-room always commence shyin' pillows in the morning, and I'm as sleepy as Rip Van Winkle. I'll have another forty winks."

"Nonsense," said Ronald, looking at his watch; "it's about seven; go and have your bath and join me on deck."

"All roight," assented Pat, with a gigantic yawn; "I daresay cold water will wake me up."

"And, I say," called out Monteith, as Pat rolled along towards the saloon, "knock up Ventin; his cabin is No. 43."

"Roight you are," from Pat, as he disappeared.

Ronald took a turn along to the end of the hurricane deck and, after surveying the slumbering forms in the smoking-room, walked back again. Just as he got to the captain's cabin he saw a steward emerge therefrom with horror and alarm on his face.

"Hullo," said the Australian, stopping short; "what's up?"

"Oh, sir," gasped the steward, pausing a moment, "Mr. Ventin, sir—he's dead—murdered!" and he ran off to the cabin of the first officer.

Ronald sat down on the nearest seat and let the cigarette drop from his fingers.

Ventin—dead—murdered!

Monteith thought of the dead man's story and how he said he would never reach England alive. His presentiment of evil was right after all for his wife had fulfilled her promise, and killed him. "But she will not escape punishment," thought Ronald, "for in order to commit the crime she must have come on board."

The news was soon all over the ship, and in a short time all the passengers were on deck. The captain, the first officer, the doctor, and the purser all went along to see the body, after which the door of the cabin was locked while they deliberated over what was to be done. The excitement was intense, for no one doubted but that a murder had been committed, though no official notice had been given, and everyone was puzzling over what could have been the motive for such a crime. Only one man on board had a clue, and this was Ronald Monteith, who determined to tell the captain Ventin's strange story, and then have the ship thoroughly searched to see if the Maltese wife of the deceased could be discovered.

After breakfast, when all the passengers were gathered in excited groups talking over the affair, Monteith went along and asking permission to see the captain on the subject, told him everything, while the doctor went down to make an examination of the body.

As the weather was very hot, the corpse would have to be buried before arrival at Gibraltar, and Captain Templeton determined to hold an inquest at once. A jury was chosen from the passengers, and the captain acted as coroner, while the witnesses were the steward, who had discovered the body, the doctor, and Ronald Monteith.

The jury, having inspected the body, went into the captain's cabin to hold the inquest, and the proceedings were opened by a speech from Captain Templeton.

He stated that a crime had been committed on board the ship, and it behoved every passenger to use his or her best energies to find out who had committed it. The idea of suicide had been talked about, but they would hear from the evidence of Mr. Monteith, an intimate friend of the deceased, that the dead man had distinctly denied having any such idea. He went to bed the previous night at half-past eight, and at seven that morning one of the stewards, by name Matthew Dalton, had gone to the deceased's cabin and found him lying dead with a stiletto in his heart. The stiletto would be laid before the jury, the evidence of the steward, the doctor, and of Mr. Monteith taken, and every attempt would be made to find the author of this dastardly crime.

The first witness called was Dalton, who deposed that he had knocked at the door of the deceased at seven as usual, but receiving no reply had entered, and found him lying in the lower berth, with a stiletto (produced) in his breast. He was completely dressed, and as all the furniture of the cabin was in order, there was no sign of any struggle.

The stiletto produced was a slender, steel instrument, about seven inches long, with a curiously carved ivory handle, representing the head of Bacchus, surrounded by clusters of grapes.

Captain: Were the bed-clothes in the berth disarranged?

Witness: No sir; he was lying on top of 'em.

Captain: Quite dressed?

Witness: Yes sir; just as if he was taking a sleep afore turning in.

Captain: Any of his jewellery missing?

20

Witness: No sir; his watch was in his pocket, and two rings on his fingers.

Captain: When did you last see him alive?

Witness: Yesterday, when he came on board at Valletta.

Captain: How long was he ashore?

Witness: About an hour sir; he came back at three o'clock; he seemed upset, and asked me to get him a glass of brandy.

Captain: Do you know what time he went to bed?

Witness: No sir.

Captain: Was there any blood about the cabin?

Witness: No sir; just a little oozing from his breast.

The doctor was next called upon to give his evidence, and deposed that he had examined the body of Lionel Ventin, deceased. It was that of a man of thirty-seven, or thereabouts, well nourished; very little food in the stomach, but a faint spirituous odour, which showed that the deceased must have been drinking previously to his death. The deceased had died from a stab inflicted by a stiletto, which had penetrated the heart. The stiletto was in the wound when the body was discovered.

Captain: At what time do you think the crime was committed?

Doctor: That is difficult to say; it was quite cold when I felt it, at seven this morning. I should say at least eight or nine hours.

Captain: From the way the wound was inflicted, did the idea of suicide occur to you?

Doctor: No; the stiletto was long, and as the body was lying in a lower compartment, he could not have lifted the stiletto high enough to have driven it so deeply, without knocking his hand against the bottom of the top berth.

Captain: If he had managed to do so, would there be any bruise or mark on his hand?

Doctor: I should say very likely; but I did not discover any.

Captain: Was there much blood?

Doctor: Very little; the stiletto had been driven into the heart and left there, so comparatively little blood could ooze out.

This closed the evidence of the doctor, and then Ronald Monteith stepped forward and told the jury the story of the deceased.

Captain: You say the deceased expected to be killed by his wife?

Monteith: He told me so several times.

Captain: And did he ever say he would commit suicide?

Monteith: He distinctly denied having any such intention.

Captain: When did you see him last?

Monteith: At half-past eight last night; he said he would go to bed early.

Captain: Was he excited in any way?

Monteith: No; just the same as usual.

Captain: If your theory is correct, and the deceased was murdered by his wife, as he expected to be, do you think she came on board at Valletta?

Monteith: Yes; I am sure of it. (Sensation.)

Captain: Will you give us your reasons?

Monteith: The deceased saw his wife in Malta, and she recognised him. When he left me at half-past eight to go to his cabin, there was a number of strangers on board; if his wife were on board, she could easily have followed him to his cabin and killed him.

Captain: But she would not know the number of his cabin?

Monteith: Yes, she would. He asked me to see him in the morning, and told me the number of his cabin twice; the second time he spoke so loudly, that anyone could have heard, and immediately afterwards went away.

Captain: Then you think the crime was committed before the sailing of the ship?

Monteith: I can't say; if, as the doctor says, the deceased had been dead for nine hours, this would bring the time of the commission of the crime to nine o'clock last night, at which time the ship sailed.

The captain asked Monteith a few other questions, and then the inquest was adjourned till the next morning.

CHAPTER IV

THE NEW PASSENGERS

When the inquest had been adjourned, and the excited passengers were assembled in saloon and smoking-rooms giving their ideas on the subject, Ronald Monteith, at the captain's request, remained to talk over things.

"It is a curious case altogether," said Captain Templeton, sitting back in his chair. "I never knew of such a thing to occur aboard one of our steamers before, and your story is a strange one."

"It is, rather," assented the Australian, pulling moodily at his mustache; "but I think it is true. Poor Ventin told me it only too bitterly to leave any doubt in my mind as to his veracity."

The captain took up the stiletto, which still lay on the table, and looked at it thoughtfully.

"Have you ever seen this in Ventin's possession?" he asked.

"No," replied Monteith, casting a careless glance at it. "But, then, I never was in his cabin. We sat next to one another in the saloon at meals, and talked together a good deal. Beyond the story I told you I know nothing about his life."

"Excuse me putting the question to you again; but do you really think this Maltese wife killed him?"

"Well, of course, I can't say for certain, but it looks very black against her. She wrote and told him she would kill him."

"Oh!" interrupted the captain, "did he show you the letter?"

"No; but it might be among his private papers, which you will of course take charge of."

"Yes; I will look over his things to-night. But go on."

"Well, he goes on shore at Valletta, sees his wife, who recognises him, comes back, she follows, hears the number of his cabin, and kills him."

"And then?"

"Well, the question is easy to answer. She must have committed the crime before nine o'clock, and escaped on shore in the confusion, or——"

"Well."

"She must be still on the boat. What passengers came on board at Valletta?"

"I ascertained that when I heard your story this morning—two only."

"Maltese or English?"

"The former. Marchese Matteo Vassalla is the name of one, and the other is Miss Cotoner—both cousins."

"Do you think she is the wife of Ventin?" asked Ronald, eagerly.

"How the deuce do I know?" said Templeton, quickly; "I never saw her before!"

"What age should you think she was?"

"About twenty-four or five."

"Women's appearances are so deceptive."

"What the deuce are you driving at?" asked the captain, annoyed.

"I know the exact age of the Maltese wife."

"How so?"

"Ventin told me he was forty years of age, and that he was twenty when he started his career in London; he said he had thirteen years of fast living there, so in order to be forty now, seven years must have elapsed since his marriage."

"But what has this got to do with the age of his wife?"

"Everything; he said his wife was twenty-three years of age when he met her first; that by my argument must have been seven years ago, so to-day his wife must be thirty years of age—now is this new passenger thirty?"

"No, I'm certain she isn't; besides, the Marchese told me his cousin and himself stayed on deck till the vessel started."

"Oh!" said Ronald, thoughtfully, "so that disposes of this young lady, it cannot be she, but the Marchese might help us."

"I don't think so; he wouldn't know Ventin."

"Perhaps not, but he might know Mrs. Ventin, as he lives at Valletta, and the whole affair might be sifted to the bottom; but oh hang it, I forgot," broke off Monteith in dismay, "Ventin was not his real name."

"Heavens, you don't say so! Then what was it?"

"He did not tell me."

"How vexatious," said Templeton, rising to his feet, "this involves the affair in still deeper mystery, for if Ventin were not his real name, we cannot find the former Mrs. Ventin, and will not be able to ascertain if there's any truth in the story he told you."

"Examine his boxes," suggested Ronald, as he followed the captain outside, "his real name may be among his papers, or else a crest; you might find out from that."

The captain jumped at the idea, and was going down to carry it into effect, when Ronald stopped him.

"I say," he asked, eagerly, "who is that pretty girl with the dark hair?"

24

"Oh that," said Templeton, with a laugh, "is the object of your suspicions, Miss Cotoner."

Captain Templeton turned away, and Ronald discovered the young lady in question was the very one he had seen on the Barraca, and of whose face he had been dreaming ever since. She, guilty of a crime? The thought was madness; if any one even hinted at such a thing, he'd throw him over the side, and he no longer was astonished at the captain's indignation at his suggestion. The fact was, Master Ronald was in the first stage of that universal disease called love. He approached Mrs. Pellypop as she sat knitting industriously, and took a seat beside her; of course, she commenced on the great subject of the day, and expressed her opinion that it was a "lascar."

"But what motive?" asked Ronald, absently; "couldn't be robbery—nothing was stolen."

"Then it must have been a steward," said Mrs. Pellypop, determinedly. "Mr. Ventin looked like a man with a temper, and very likely struck a steward, who retaliated by killing him—oh, it's as clear as day to me."

"But where did he get his weapon?" asked Ronald.

"Stole it from the plate basket," said Mrs. Pellypop, whose idea of stilettos was vague.

"It was not a table knife," began Ronald, then broke off suddenly as he saw Miss Cotoner move away with a tall, slender, dark man. "I say, Mrs. Pellypop, who's that?"

"Whom?" asked Mrs. Pellypop, putting up her glasses. "Oh, the girl from Malta?"

"No not Miss Cotoner, I know who she is; but the fellow?"

"Oh, her cousin, the Marchese Vassalla," answered Mrs. Pellypop; "not that I care much for foreign titles myself, but he looks a gentleman."

And, as a matter of fact, he was by no means ill-looking, but when Ronald saw him he instantly took a dislike to him. Why, he did not know, unless it was on the Dr. Fell principle; it might have been instinct, perhaps prejudice; but the fact remained nevertheless—he did not like Matteo Vassalla. A handsome face certainly, with swarthy skin, brilliant, black eyes, and a coal black beard carefully trimmed. In his slender, sinewy figure there was something of the lithe grace of a panther; and what with the graceful movements of his hands, and the deferential manner with which he bent towards Miss Cotoner, he decidedly did not impress Monteith favourably.

But the lady—well, she has been described before, and as Ronald looked at her he only found new perfections. She had rather

25

a sad expression on her face, and her head was a little bent down, but, for the rest, she was as straight and graceful as Artemis. Ronald, who had stoutly resisted all the blandishments of the pretty girls on board, caught one glance of those brilliantly black eyes and surrendered at once. He also caught the glance of another pair of eyes which did not regard him in such a friendly manner, and drew himself up haughtily as he left Mrs. Pellypop, and went down to the saloon.

"What the deuce did that foreign cad mean by staring at me like that;" he muttered, quite forgetting that the cad in question had a title, and was of higher rank than himself; "I don't suppose he has anything to do with her; perhaps they are engaged—hang it, it's impossible, she'd never throw herself away on a thing like that. I'll ask old mother Pellypop to-morrow, she'll be sure to know all about her in that time."

Having thus, in his own mind, satisfactorily settled the affair, Ronald went down to his cabin to dress for dinner.

Meanwhile Miss Cotoner and her cousin were having a few words on the subject of Mr. Monteith.

"What a handsome man," said Miss Cotoner, following the tall figure of the Australian with her eyes.

"Bah! a beef-eating Englishman," retorted Vassalla, with an angry light in his wicked black eyes, "he has no brain."

"You've to find that out yet," retorted the young lady, who seemed to take delight in tormenting her companion. "I think he's charming. I'm sure he looks it; I saw him yesterday on the Barraca."

"Remember you are engaged to me," replied the Marchese, angrily.

"By my parents, yes," she replied, coldly; "but not with my own consent."

"Consent, bah! let wiser heads guide yours, Carmela."

"Well, I certainly would not ask your head to take the position," replied Carmela, contemptuously. "Why do you annoy me like this; do you think I left my sister only to be worried by you? No, I don't think so, there is too much of the frying-pan into the fire theory in that for me."

"I will get your sister to take you back," he said, vindictively.

"Oh no, you won't," she retorted, turning on him; "I'm of age—my own mistress, and I have elected to go and stop with my cousins in England. If I choose to marry an Englishman I certainly will in spite of your threats; so good-bye Matteo, I'm going to dress for dinner," and she walked gracefully away, leaving the Marchese in a delightful temper.

"Bah!" he muttered angrily to himself, "she is only a woman;

26

patience my good Matteo, you shall win her yet, and then——." He closed his mouth with an angry snap that did not argue well for the happiness of Miss Cotoner's future life.

"What a flirt that girl is," thought Mrs. Pellypop, as she looked after the young lady; "I'm sure I don't know what the world is coming to; I never flirted," and to Mrs. Pellypop's credit, it must be said, she never had, but then, as Rochefoucauld remarks, some women are safe because nobody seeks after them.

When Ronald emerged from his cabin in evening dress, he was caught at the foot of the stairs by Pat, who, in company with a few convivial spirits, was having a sherry and bitters.

"Come and have something to drink after all your labours," he said, in a hospitable manner; "anything new about the affair?"

"No, I don't think so," replied Ronald sadly; "poor Ventin! To think he was so jolly last night and now dead."

"Do you think the person who killed him is on board?" asked Pat, confidentially.

"No I don't," retorted Ronald, decisively; "I believe she's to be found at Malta, and I'll hunt her down and punish her somehow."

"Why?"

"Because I liked Ventin—he had a miserable life, and a miserable end, and a wicked woman like that wife of his is not fit to live."

"Stop a bit old boy," observed Pat, coolly, "you haven't brought the crime home to her yet."

"But I will," reiterated Monteith, doggedly; "I'm sure it's she, and if it isn't, I'll make it my business in life to find out who is the criminal."

"I say Monteith," said Bentley, a vacuous-looking youth with no brains and lots of money, "Ventin's place was next to you at table— who are they going to put there?"

"I don't know and I don't care," growled Ronald, savagely turning away, cursing Mr. Bentley under his breath for his callous way of speaking.

"Seems cut up," lisped Bentley, putting up his eye-glass in nowise disturbed.

"Well, it's no joke having a fellow you like murdered," said Pat, finishing his sherry; "and Ventin was a good sort anyhow."

Then they all commenced talking again about the mystery till Pat grew weary of the discussion, and went on deck, where he found Ronald leaning over the side looking moodily at the water.

"Well old chap," said Pat, slapping him on the shoulder, "don't take it so much to heart."

27

"It wasn't that," replied Monteith; "I was thinking how we could find out his real name."

"Why, wasn't it Ventin?"

"He said it wasn't."

"Search his baggage."

"That's been done, but without result—all his linen is marked L. V., all his letters directed to Lionel Ventin, in fact, it's the only name that can be found."

"Then it must be his real name," asserted Pat.

"Not necessarily; he told me he changed his name, so he evidently did it thoroughly."

"Any crest—that might give a clue?"

"No, nothing."

"Oh! it seems a deuce of a muddle. Hullo, there's the dinner bell—come down old boy, I'm starving."

They went below, and found nearly all the tables full. Pat went to his own table, and Ronald sat sadly down by the side of Ventin's empty chair. He was not there very long when he heard a rustle, and on turning round saw that Miss Cotoner was sitting beside him. Yes, sitting in the dead man's chair, so with a sudden impulse Ronald arose.

"I beg your pardon," he said, bowing; "but would you mind taking my chair instead of that one?"

"Why?" asked the young lady coldly.

"Because—because," he stammered, confusedly, "it was Mr.—Mr. Ventin's, the gentleman who died."

"Oh!" she said, and turned rather pale, "thank you"—rising—"I will accept your offer," and she sat in Monteith's chair while he took poor Ventin's.

Of course this little incident was observed by all, and by none more so than Matteo Vassalla, who sat at a distant table, and looked remarkably savage.

"Wait a little," he muttered; "when you are mine, I'll tame you."

Pat, indicating Ronald and Miss Cotoner to Kate Lester, hummed the first line of his favourite song, "I love a lubly gal I do."

"What do you think?" he asked.

Miss Lester laughed and nodded.

"I think the same as you," she answered.

28

CHAPTER V

A DAY AT "GIB"

THE inquest on the body of Lionel Ventin was resumed next day, but nothing new was discovered, and taking into consideration the strange story told by the deceased to Monteith, the time of the committal of the crime, which, according to the Doctor's showing, must have taken place when the ship was leaving Valletta, there appeared no doubt but that the murder had been committed before the steamer left Malta. As the deceased's real name was not Ventin, and all the evidence was purely circumstantial, the jury brought in a verdict of "Wilful murder against a person unknown." The evidence was taken down so as to be handed to the authorities in Gibraltar, entries were made in the log-book about the affair, and poor Lionel Ventin's body was committed to the deep.

There is something inexpressibly sorrowful and solemn in a burial at sea. The body, wrapped in a sail, with iron shot at its feet, was placed on the lower deck near the open bulwarks, and was covered with the Union Jack. A number of the passengers were present, leaning from the upper deck, but many of the ladies, among whom was Mrs. Pellypop, were reading the service for the dead to themselves in the saloon. The captain, surrounded by his officers, read the service over the deceased, and at a signal the body was pushed over the side, slipping from under the Union Jack, and fell with a dull splash into the sea. Then everyone dispersed, the engines, which had been slowed down during the burial, resumed their usual speed, and life on board went on as usual. There was a gloom, however, over all the ship, for it was not an ordinary death, and it was not until the "Neptune" reached Gibraltar that the passengers began to recover their usual gaiety.

Meanwhile Ronald Monteith had become the slave of Carmela Cotoner, and, judging from her gracious manner towards him, she was in no wise displeased at having him at her feet. Ronald had hitherto laughed at the tender passion, but now he was being paid back for insulting the god of Love, as he found out to his cost. He was always at Carmela's elbow—carried her rugs and pillows about for her, danced with her, read poetry to her, and, in fact, was so constant in his attentions, that it was soon patent to the whole ship that Monteith was madly in love with the girl from Malta.

And, indeed, she was called nothing else. Mrs. Pellypop, not knowing her name at first, had given her that title, and everyone else followed suit. She was the belle of the ship, vice Kate Lester resigned, and was always followed by an adoring crowd of young men, of whom Ronald grew unspeakably jealous, and would get quite sulky if she smiled or spoke to anyone else. He carried this absurd behaviour to such an extent that Pat Ryan took him to task one day for his sins.

"You are a jolly old ass, Ronald," observed the candid Irishman, "to go on like this, making a fool of yourself."

"I can't help it," said Monteith, ruefully surveying at a distance a group of young fellows standing round Carmela; "just look at her; she doesn't care a bit about me."

"Of course, you say that," said Pat, lighting a cigarette, "because she doesn't devote herself exclusively to you. I tell ye what, girls don't like being made faces at because they speak to another fellow; hang it, I've seen you speak to girls enough."

"That was before I—I," hesitatingly, "met Miss Cotoner."

"Before you were in love, ye mean," retorted Pat; "begad, ye've got the disease badly. Are ye going to marry her?"

"I will, if she'll have me."

"Then why don't you ask her?"

"I've only known her a few days. Isn't that rather soon?"

"Not a bit, women like to be taken by storm," wisely remarked Pat, who was just out of the nursery, and fancied he knew the sex—Heaven help him—"go in, and win, my boy."

"By Jove I will," said Ronald, eagerly, and then fell to thinking what his father would say to the marriage. He didn't know who the young lady was—what she was—knew nothing about her family, and yet—and yet, he adored her. Why shouldn't he marry her? He was his own master, and if his father cut him off with a shilling, he could work—she was worth working for—yes, he would ask her to marry him—of course she would say yes—for it never entered this confident young man's head that women sometimes say "No." So Master Ronald went on building castles in the air, all inhabited by himself and Mrs. Monteith—no hang it, not yet—the girl from Malta.

He was aroused from these golden visions by a touch on his arm, and turning round, saw his special dislike, the Marchese Vassalla, looking at him. The Marchese detested Monteith, both for his good looks, and for the evident regard Miss Cotoner had for him. He would like to have dropped his rival over the side along with poor Ventin's body, but as he couldn't do this, he was excessively polite, and watched for an opportunity to do him an injury. Here was a chance now, and the wily Maltese took full advantage of it. He

30

overheard the conversation between Pat and Monteith, so determined to dash all Ronald's hopes to the ground, by telling him that Carmela was engaged. To this end the serpent came into Ronald's paradise, and smiling, invited him not to have an apple, but a drink. The young man would have refused, but then he thought he might learn something about Carmela, and after all, the Marchese was her cousin, so he consented, and went down to the bar with the smiling Maltese gentleman.

As it was about eleven o'clock, they found the bar surrounded by thirsty souls having cocktails. In fact, there was a "Cocktail Club" on board, and it was a very popular drink with the young men, particularly if they had been up late the night before. Cocktails therefore, being the prevailing beverage, the Marchese and his victim each had one, and then the former gentleman opened the campaign.

"I shall be sorry when this voyage is over," he said, carelessly.

"So shall I," replied Monteith, thinking of the chances of meeting Carmela in London. "But I daresay I'll meet Miss—I mean you again."

"I don't think so," said Vassalla, coldly. "Myself and my cousin only stay a few days in London, and then go down to some friends in the country."

"Oh!" said Ronald, and looked blank.

"And then," pursued his tormentor, eyeing him mercilessly, "I am coming back to London to arrange about our marriage."

The poor lad turned pale as death.

"Whose marriage?"

"Mine and my cousin's. Did you not know we were engaged?"

Ronald finished his drink in a mechanical sort of way, and putting down his glass, walked away to his cabin, and shut himself in. The Marchese looked after him with a grim smile.

"I think that will give you food for reflection my friend," he muttered, lighting a cigarette as he strolled away.

"What's up with that Maltese devil?" asked Bentley. "He looks quite pleased with himself."

"It's more than Monteith did; he walked away as pale as a ghost," said Pat.

"It's about the girl from Malta, you bet," said Bentley, sagely, and no one contradicted him.

Miss Cotoner was without her attentive cavalier all that day, and was much surprised thereat. She asked her cousin about him, and that smiling gentleman told her Ronald was ill, and had gone to lie down. And indeed, Ronald was ill, not with a headache, but with a heart-ache, which is worse, and he lay all day in his narrow berth

31

bemoaning his hard fate. Nor did he come to dinner, and Miss Cotoner was so vexed to think he was so ill, that she sent her steward with a little note to his cabin, saying how sorry she was, and she hoped he would be well enough on the morrow to take her over Gibraltar, all of which Monteith read and puzzled over.

"She's a flirt, a heartless coquette," cried the poor boy; "she's engaged to another man, and she's trying to break my heart, but she won't. I care no more for her than this bit of paper," and he threw the little note on the floor.

After a bit, however—with the usual inconsistency of lovers—he picked it up, and thought what a pretty hand she wrote, and then that he would go over Gibraltar with her, and he would find out if she were really engaged to that beastly Maltese. Ronald's language was strong but not choice. Then he sent a reply to Carmela, saying he would see her in the morning, and afterwards drank a bottle of champagne, and felt better. Oh what a queer disease is love, with its hopes, its fears, its smiles and tears, its kisses and blisses, and—its intense egotism.

The next day Monteith arose, cooled his hot head with a shower bath, donned a suit of spotless, white flannels, put a straw hat on his curly locks, and sallied forth with the determination to save his charming Princess from the clutches of the ogre Vassalla, or die in the attempt.

"Hullo," cried Pat, seeing the unusual splendour of Master Ronald's apparel, "going on the mash to-day? gad you'll knock the Gib girls over like nine-pins."

Whereat Ronald informed Pat in confidence that he intended to try his fate with Miss Cotoner that day, and Pat informed Ronald, likewise in confidence, that he thought he was quite right, and would bet him a bottle of champagne he would be accepted, which wager Monteith took, and went on deck with a light heart and a strong determination to win. All this time, however, in spite of his new-born love, Monteith never for a moment wavered from his determination to hunt down the assassin of his dead friend, and told Captain Templeton as much.

"How are you going to do it?" asked Templeton, dubiously, "we cannot even find out Ventin's real name."

"Isn't there a portrait of him among his luggage?" asked Monteith. Templeton shook his head.

"Not anything likely to lead to identification," he answered, "but I'll have a talk with you after we leave Gibraltar, for I must confess I would like the riddle solved," and the captain went off to his post on the bridge as they were now nearing the famous Rock.

Who that has once seen it can forget that enormous grey mass

32

rising up from the blue water into the blue sky, with the red-roofed town nestling at its base? Monteith had never seen anything so impressive since Aden, which he had beheld, vague and mysterious, in the starlight. He realized with a thrill of pride that this was one of the visible signs of England's greatness, and he thought, with satisfaction, that he, too, was of the race that had conquered it. Aden, Malta, Gibraltar, all held by England; it made Ronald quite patriotic when he thought of the impregnability of these strongholds. If he had been a poet he would have burst into verse, but as he was not he simply contented himself with a commonplace observation—

"By Jove, it's wonderful!"

The Anglo-Saxon race are rarely enthusiastic.

The ship cast anchor about a mile from the shore, and soon Ronald and his beloved were in one of the boats dancing over the choppy water. Pat also was in the boat, and so was Mrs. Pellypop and Kate Lester. Ronald hinted to Pat that the old lady would be in the way, but Pat magnanimously said he would look after both her and Miss Lester, so as to leave Monteith free to pursue his wooing with Carmela.

When they reached shore, they rejected all the offers of carriages made by brown-skinned natives of the Rock, and sauntered leisurely up the dusty street, under the massive gateway above which they could see the red-coated sentries, and walked right into the market-place, where a lot of buying, selling, swindling, and talking were going on. Jews, with black, beady eyes and hooked noses, invited them into dingy little shops and produced oriental goods; and sedate-looking Moors in baggy trousers and large turbans, watched them, with Eastern apathy, as they passed along. The tall white houses with the striped awnings over the windows, the crowd of dirty little brats howling for money, the number of red uniforms about, and the narrow, crowded streets, all afforded them much amusement. Then Mrs. Pellypop, inveigled by the wily Pat, went into a shop to buy some things, and was soon engaged in a lively altercation with the shopman, who spoke broken English, and showed her broken things which he said came from Granada, and would have had a broken head if Mrs. Pellypop had not reflected that using her umbrella for such a purpose, might lower her dignity. Pat and Miss Lester looked on and laughed at the scene, so, taking advantage of the confusion, Ronald and Carmela slipped away and climbed up the steep lanes to the old Moorish castle which frowns over the town.

"I don't care much for ruins," said Miss Cotoner, putting up her red sunshade, and a pretty picture she looked under it; "there's a good deal of sameness about them; but Moorish architecture is picturesque."

"Yes, very!" assented Ronald, who would have agreed to anything she said.

"I have Arab blood in my own veins," observed Carmela; "at least, so my father said. One of our ancestors was an Emir."

"Is your father alive?" asked Ronald, who saw in this remark a good opportunity for finding out all about his beloved.

"No, he died a long time ago," she said, sadly. "My mother is also dead, and I lived in Malta with my sister."

"Was that your sister who was with you the first time I saw you?"

Carmela nodded.

"Yes, we did not get on well together, so I left her and am going to some relations in England."

"Then I shall not see you again," said the young man, in a moody tone.

"That depends on yourself," she replied, blushing.

All the blood rushed to Ronald's fair face, and it was only by a great effort he prevented himself from taking her in his arms, and kissing her.

"Does your cousin, the Marchese go with you?" he asked eagerly.

"I believe so."

"I suppose you are glad?"

"Glad!" she looked at him with surprise; "why on earth should I be glad?"

"Because—because—well"—desperately—"he's going to marry you."

Carmela frowned.

"Who told you so?"

"Vassalla himself—is it true?" asked the young man breathlessly.

Miss Cotoner looked at him in a queer manner for a moment, then turned away her head.

"My parents arranged a match between us," she answered, nervously.

"And you?"

"I'm not in favour of it—I don't think there is any chance of my ever marrying the Marchese."

Ronald sprang forward with a cry of delight.

"Oh, Miss Cotoner—Carmela—I——"

"Would like to see the fortifications," she answered, quickly

34

nipping the declaration, she knew was coming, in the bud; "I wouldn't; let us go down to the Almeda."

She turned away, and Ronald followed mortified and humbled at his failure, but half way down the hill began to pick up his spirits.

"I can't expect her to fall like ripe fruit into my mouth," he thought, hopefully; "and it's impossible she can love me in so short a time."

He was wrong there, for Carmela liked him very much—in fact, more than she cared to acknowledge to herself; but she would not allow him to speak because—well, because she was a riddle. Woman is an eternal riddle that man has been trying to solve since the beginning of the world, but every attempt has failed.

Monteith, however, took his failure like the honest gentleman he was, and turned the conversation. Remembering his anxiety to solve the mystery of Ventin's death, he thought he would question his fair companion. "Did you know a lady in Valletta called Mrs. Ventin?" he asked, as they walked slowly along in the burning sun.

"No, I never heard the name before," replied Carmela promptly, looking at him.

"Of course not," thought Monteith; "it wasn't his right name."

"Who is she?" said Carmela carelessly; "that's the same name as the gentleman who died."

"She was his wife," replied Ronald.

"Does she live at Valletta?" asked Miss Cotoner.

"I think so."

"Strange I never met her."

"She was married to my friend seven years ago."

"Oh!" said Miss Cotoner with a slight start; "no I never heard of her, Mr. Monteith."

They were strolling along the Almeda by this time, and the Grand Promenade of Gibraltar was crowded. Many an admiring glance was directed at the pretty girl Ronald as escorting; and one young officer was heard to declare that "That dark girl was deuced good style you know."

On the Almeda they met Mrs. Pellypop, and the ever-lively Pat along with Miss Lester, and the whole party were tired and dusty with sight-seeing. Mrs. Pellypop, in fact, was rather cross, but triumphant, as she had secured a number of bargains, though, truth to tell, she had paid dearly for her purchases. She was not at all pleased at seeing Ronald escorting Carmela, and observed, with some asperity, that it was time to return to the ship. Everyone being weary agreed, and they went down the steep street out of the gate, and Pat ran to get a boat. While thus waiting, the Marchese Vassalla came up and addressed himself with some anger to Miss Cotoner.

"I did not get on shore till you left, and have been looking for you all day; you ought to have waited for me to escort you."

"Thank you," replied his cousin languidly; "Mr. Monteith has been kind enough to relieve you of your duties."

The look Vassalla cast on Ronald was not, by any means, a pleasant one.

CHAPTER VI

MRS. PELLYPOP TALKS

Mrs. Pellypop was an epitome of all that was good; a happy mixture of Hannah More and Florence Nightingale, with just a slight flavour of Mrs. Candour to add piquancy to her character. She was an excellent housekeeper, a devout Christian, rigorous in all her social duties, a faithful wife—and yet, the late Mr. Pellypop must have been glad when he died. She was too overpoweringly virtuous, and wherever she went showed herself such a shining example of all that was excellent, that she made everyone else's conduct, however proper it might be, look black beside her own. The fact is, people do not like playing second fiddle, and as Mrs. Pellypop always insisted on leading the social orchestra, her room was regarded as better than her company.

Her father had been a clergyman, and when she married Mr. Pellypop, who was in the wine trade, and came out to Melbourne to settle, she never lost an opportunity of acquainting people with the fact. Mr. Pellypop died from an overdose of respectability, and left his widow fairly well off, so she declined to marry again—not having any chance of doing so—and devoted herself to the education of her only daughter, Elizabeth, whom she nearly succeeded in making as objectionably genteel as herself. Elizabeth was good, gentle, and meek, and as Mrs. Pellypop wanted a son-in-law of a similar nature, she married Elizabeth to the Rev. Charles Mango, who was then a humble curate in Melbourne.

After marriage, the Rev. Charles turned out to have a will of his own, and refused to let Mrs. Pellypop manage his household as she wished to do. Indeed, when he was created Bishop of Patagonia for his book on "Missionary Mistakes," he went off with his meek little wife to his diocese in South America, and absolutely refused to let his upright mother-in-law accompany him. So Mrs. Pellypop made a virtue of necessity, and stayed behind in Melbourne; talked scandal with her small circle of friends, bragged about her son-in-law the Bishop, gave tracts to the poor, which they did not want, and refused them money, which they did, and, in short, led, as she thought, a useful, Christian life. Other people said she was meddlesome, but then we all have our enemies, and if the rest of her sex could not be as noble and virtuous as Mrs. Pellypop, why it was their own fault.

37

At last she heard that the Bishop and his wife had gone to England to see that worthy prelate's parents, so Mrs. Pellypop sold all her carefully preserved furniture, gave up her house, and took her passage on board the "Neptune" in order to see her dear children before they went back to the wilds of South America. On board the ship she asserted her authority at once, and came a kind of female Alexander Selkirk, monarch of all she surveyed. Two or three ladies did indeed attempt a feeble resistance, but Mrs. Pellypop made a good fight for it, and soon reduced them to submission. Her freezing glance, like that of Medusa, turned everyone into stone, and though the young folk talked flippantly enough about her behind her back, they were quiet enough under the mastery of her eye.

When the ship left Gibraltar, late in the afternoon, Mrs. Pellypop was not pleased, and sat in her deck chair steadily knitting, and frowned at the grand mass of the Ape's Head on the African coast as if that mountain had seriously displeased her. She was annoyed with the conduct of Miss Cotoner who took an independent stand and refused to be dictated to by Mrs. Pellypop or anyone else; so the good lady, anxious to guide the young and impulsive girl, and find out all about her, determined to speak to her and subjugate her, if possible. So she sat in her chair knitting away like one of the Fates, and pondering over her plan of action, for Mrs. Pellypop never did anything in hurry, and always marshalled her forces beforehand.

Carmela, with the Marchese on one side and Ronald on the other—both of which gentlemen were exchanging scowls of hate—was looking at the romantic coast of Spain as they steamed through the Straits. The rolling, green meadows—undulating, like the waves of the sea, with the glint of yellow sunlight on them made a charming picture, and, turning to the other side, she could see the granite peaks of the Ape's Head with wreaths of feathery clouds round it, and, a little farther back, the white houses of Ceuta. Add to this charming view, a bright sky, a fresh breeze, which made the white sails belly out before it, and two delightful young men to talk to, it was little to be wondered at that Carmela felt happy.

"So these are the Pillars of Hercules?" she said, looking from one side of the strait to the other.

"Yes," answered her cousin, "so the Greeks said. I don't think much of Hercules as an architect—do you?"

"Indeed I do," replied Carmela, enthusiastically; "what can be grander than Gibraltar and the Ape's Head?"

"They are not exactly alike," said Ronald, looking at Vassalla, "and the Marchese likes consistency."

"Of course, I do," retorted Vassalla, with an angry flush on his cheek, "especially in women," with a significant look at his cousin.

"Then my dear Matteo, you are sure to be disappointed," retorted Miss Cotoner, calmly, "for you'll never get it—the age of miracles is past my friend."

Ronald laughed, and was rewarded by a scowl from the Marchese, and then Carmela, tired of keeping peace between these hot-headed young men, went off to talk to Mrs. Pellypop. Without doubt, there would have been high words between the rivals had not a steward come up to Ronald with a message that the captain wanted to see him. So Ronald retreated, leaving Vassalla in possession of the field, and the Marchese, seeing there was no chance of talking to Carmela, went off to solace himself with a cigarette.

Meanwhile, Mrs. Pellypop received Carmela with an affectation of friendliness, and proceeded to question her in a Machiavellian manner.

"What a pretty place Valletta is," said the matron, dropping her knitting and rubbing her plump white lands; "I suppose you know it very well?"

"I ought to," answered the girl laughing; "I've lived there nearly all my life."

"Yet you speak English well," said Mrs. Pellypop sceptically.

"Yes, there are so many English people in Malta; and, besides, my mother was English."

"Oh," thought Mrs. Pellypop, noticing the use of the past tense, "her mother is dead." "So you are going home to your mother's people I suppose?" she asked aloud.

"Just on a visit," replied Carmela carelessly.

"Indeed, they live in London I presume?"

"No, at Marlow on the Thames."

"Oh!" said Mrs. Pellypop, sitting up suddenly, "is that so? I am going down there myself on a visit to my son-in-law. He's the Bishop of Patagonia, my dear, and his parents live near Marlow. Mango is the name. I believe they are well known."

"Yes; I've heard of them," said Carmela cordially. "A dear old couple I believe."

Mrs. Pellypop drew herself up stiffly: "The parents of a bishop should never be called 'a dear old couple';" it savoured of the peasantry.

"May I inquire the name of your relative?" she asked, coldly, taking up her knitting.

"Sir Mark Trevor."

"Indeed," said Mrs. Pellypop, impressed with the fact that the young lady was connected with a baronet. "It's a Cornish name, is it not?"

"I believe so. He has estates in Cornwall; but also has a house on the Thames, where he stays for the summer."

"Oh! a bachelor's place I presume?" said Mrs. Pellypop artfully.

"Not exactly; he's a widower, and has one daughter nearly as old as I am, and they are going to meet me London, and then we intend to go to Marlow for the summer."

"Then I shall probably see you there," said Mrs. Pellypop cordially.

"It's not unlikely," replied Carmela rising. "Good-bye, for the present, Mrs. Pellypop, I'm going to lie down for an hour before dinner."

"Good-bye, my dear," said the matron, resuming her knitting. "I hope I shall meet you on the Thames. I should like you to know the bishop."

Carmela laughed as she went downstairs.

"She's quite pleased with me now," she said gaily; "and all because I have a cousin who is a baronet. Heavens, how amusing these people are!"

Mrs. Pellypop was pleased with Miss Cotoner; and what she had termed forward conduct before, she now called eccentricity. This young lady had aristocratic relatives, which relatives lived near the place to which Mrs. Pellypop was going. So the worthy matron, who had a slight spice of worldliness, resolved to cultivate the girl from Malta as a desirable acquaintance.

"She needs a mother's care," thought good Mrs. Pellypop, "so I must try and look after her."

What would Mrs. Pellypop's conduct have been had Carmela told her that her cousin was a butcher? Just the same of course; for how could a good woman attach any importance to such idle things as rank and wealth?

Meanwhile Ronald was in the captain's cabin talking over the mysterious crime which had takes place on board the "Neptune;" and both of them were in considerable doubt how to proceed.

"I want the affair cleared up," said Templeton, "if only for the credit of the ship; it won't encourage people to travel with us if they think there's a chance of being murdered on board."

"The difficulty is how to start," replied Ronald thoughtfully; "you see there is absolutely no clue to follow."

"Precisely," answered the Captain leaning forward, "let me state the case. A gentleman comes on board at Melbourne, and conducts himself in a rational and sane manner, which puts the idea of suicide quite out of the question—just before we arrive at Malta he is restless and uneasy, and tells you the story of his life, which affords strong grounds for suspicion that his wife wanted to kill him—he goes on shore, spies his wife, and returns at once on board—he goes to bed before the ship sails, and the deck is crowded with all sorts and conditions of people, such a crowd that there's absolutely no chance of knowing any of them. He is found dead next morning, with an Italian stiletto in his breast, a weapon which a Maltese would probably use in preference to a knife. There is no evidence to show that anyone was seen near his cabin. Now your theory is that his wife came on board before the ship sailed, killed him, and escaped on shore in the confusion?"

"Yes; that is my theory, but only founded on the story he told me."

"Very good! We then find he told you that Ventin as not his real name. I search his boxes and papers, ad find no other name but Lionel Ventin, and yet he distinctly denied that that was his proper name?"

"He did—distinctly."

"I place all the facts and evidence in the hands of he authorities at Gibraltar, and they are equally mystified, with ourselves—they suggest that it might have been a lascar or a steward."

"Impossible! there was no motive."

"No robbery, certainly," answered Templeton; "but do you think there could have been any other motive?"

"How could there? With the exception of myself, he was very reserved with everyone else on board."

"Then we dismiss the steward and lascar theories; it must have been the wife. Now I have stated the case; how do you propose to unravel the mystery?"

"Ask me something easier," replied Ronald with laugh.

"Think again—he told you his story, did he mention any names?"

"One; Elsie Macgregor."

"Good: now do you see a clue?"

"Ah!"—Ronald thought a moment,—"yes, I see what you mean, if Ventin were divorced, Elsie Macgregor must have been joined as co-respondent."

"Exactly," answered Templeton; "I see you've caught my idea; now I can't take up this case, and though I'll have to put it into the hands of the authorities, they are sure to make a mess of it, so if you want to unravel this mystery, you must find out the murderer or murderers of Lionel Ventin yourself."

"I see," said Ronald, pulling his mustache, "you want me to find out the divorce case."

41

The Captain nodded triumphantly.

"But Macgregor is such a common name," objected Ronald; "there may be dozens of co-respondents called Macgregor."

"Very likely, but what about the sex? The co-respondent you look for must be a woman called Elsie Macgregor.

"Yes," cried Ronald, quickly, "and then I'll find out Ventin's real name."

"Of course," answered the Captain, "and once you find out his real name you'll soon find the wife."

"And then?"

Templeton shrugged his shoulders.

"Oh, then you'll have to prove the truth of his story to you."

"But if I find out all about her, the stiletto will have to be put in evidence."

"Of course," answered Templeton; "and that you can get from the authorities at Gibraltar, in whose hands I placed it."

"I have a letter of introduction to the son of an old friend of my father," said Ronald; "he is a barrister, of the Middle Temple."

"Oh—young?"

"About thirty."

"The very man," replied Templeton rising, "go and see him and tell him all about it; if he's anxious to make a mark in the world——"

"Which he hasn't done yet," interjected Ronald.

"He'll go in for this case; gad, I wish I could go into it myself; I ought to have been a private detective."

"Well," said Ronald, as they went out on to the deck; "I came for a pleasure trip, but it looks as if I shall have to work all the time."

"Yes, but think of the time you will have of it putting this puzzle together," replied Templeton, "it will be most exciting; besides, if you bring this crime home you'll get your reward; if not on earth, at least in heaven."

"I'd rather have it on earth," said Ronald, thinking of Carmela.

42

CHAPTER VII

THE END OF THE VOYAGE

There is no sadder word in the English language than "Farewell." How many quivering lips have said it with breaking hearts and scalding tears—the soldier marching away with flying banners and martial music—the emigrant sitting on deck, seeing the blue hills of the land of his birth fading away in the shadows of the night—the young man going forth into the world, and turning once more to see through tear-dimmed eyes the old house where he was born, and the lovers parting—never to meet again. Yes it is a sad word, and has caused more tears and heart-aches than any we use. Now that the voyage was coming to an end, those who had been in close companionship for nearly six weeks, knew that they must separate in a short time and, that the memory of the pleasant company on board the "Neptune" would soon be only a dream of the past. No wonder then, that as the steamer glided up the Thames, everyone was a little melancholy.

The voyage from Gibraltar had been pleasant. They had seen the famous Trafalgar Bay, where Nelson won his Waterloo—passed Cape St. Vincent in the night—caught a glimpse of the mouth of the Tagus in the early morning, and steamed safely through the Bay of Biscay, which did not act up to the reputation gained for it by the song, but was as calm as a mill-pond.

On arriving at Plymouth, some of the passengers had gone to London by rail, in preference to facing the chance of a collision in the English Channel. It was Ronald's first glimpse of England, and Chester, who was very patriotic, asked him what he thought of it?

"It's the best groomed country I've seen," said Ronald, with a smile, and, indeed, though the epithet was odd, it was very appropriate, for after all the barbaric colouring they had seen at Colombo—the arid rocks of Malta and Gibraltar, and the sandy shore of Port Said, this wonderfully, vividly green land, with fields and well-kept hedges cultivated down to the water's edge, looked, as the Australian said, "well groomed."

They anchored for about two hours at Plymouth, but there was no time to go on shore, so they gazed longingly at the quaint town so famous in English History. The Hoe—the bowling green where Sir Francis Drake played bowls when the Armada was descried "stretching out like a crescent,"—and Mount Edgecumbe, which the commander of the great fleet designed for his residence when

England was conquered. Ronald stood silent, looking at all this beauty, when a remark of Pat's made him laugh.

"I say," said Pat, mindful of Colombo and Aden, to Chester, who was quite inflated with patriotic pride, "will the people here come off, and dive for pennies?"

Chester glared at him viciously, and then stalked away too indignant to speak, while all around roared at the queerness of the remark.

"Well I thought they might," explained Pat to his grinning auditors; "the natives did it at all the other places."

"There are no natives here confound you!" said Chester, who had returned.

"Oh, indade!" replied Pat innocently, "this England's inhabited by foreigners."

After this Chester concluded to leave Pat alone.

It was night when they sailed up the Channel, and they could see in the distance the twinkling lights of Folkestone, Dover, Margate, and all the other well-known places, and as it was the last night on board, there was a general jubilation in the smoking-room after the ladies had retired. Songs were sung, toasts were proposed, speeches were made, and when the electric light was put out, candles were produced, and the concert kept up far into the night, or rather morning, One gentleman said he could play musical glasses, and broke fifteen tumblers in demonstrating his ability to do so—then they had more liquor, sang "God save the Queen," and went off to bed one by one, and everything was quiet.

And what a curious appearance the deck presented next morning—everyone in his best—no more flannel suits and straw hats, but accurate frock coats and tall hats, while the ladies came out in dresses of the newest fashions. Knots of people were talking together—giving addresses, making appointments, and promising to write, until it was queer to hear the jargon like this:—

"You won't forget—the Alhambra you know—best shop in London—lace veils cheaper than——address will always find me—Piccadilly Circus, on——cheap hotel; just off—Margate's the jolliest—Oh! the devil take the—nicest girl you ever—set foot on shore," and so on, until Ronald, who stood by Carmela, could not help laughing. The Marchese was looking after his own things, and as Ronald had his luggage in perfect order, he had Carmela all to himself.

"So this is the Thames," he said, looking at the dull, leaden stream, flowing between the dingy banks.

"The Thames of commerce, not of poetry," she corrected, smiling, "you must come down to Marlow and see the real river."

"May I?" he asked, eagerly, thinking he detected an invitation in her tones.

"Of course you may," she answered, carelessly. "I don't control your movements."

"Not at present, but you might," he replied, hurriedly.

There was an awkward pause, luckily broken by Pat, who came rushing along with his usual impetuosity.

"Ah Miss Cotoner, an' is that you?" said Pat, dolefully; "the best of friends must part, and we may niver meet again."

"We might," answered Carmela, with a laugh; "the world is small."

"Begad, I wish me heart was," said Ryan, sadly; "it's large enough to hold all the girls on board—you included."

"Much obliged," retorted the young lady, with a bow, not in the least offended, for Pat was a licensed Jester; "but I'll not consent to be one of many."

"Ye'd rayther have one honest heart?" asked Pat, looking keenly at her.

She turned his remark off with a laugh.

"Depends upon the owner of the heart," she replied, gaily.

"Ah begad thin I'm out of it," said Pat, and ran off, leaving them in exactly the same awkward situation as he found them.

"What are you going to do when you reach London?" asked Carmela after a pause, during which Ronald kept his eyes on her face.

"Many things," he answered, calmly; "first I am going to set to work to find out who killed my friend Ventin."

"I'm sure I hope you will be successful," she replied, heartily; "but why in London—the crime was committed at Malta?"

"Yes, but the motive for the crime will, I think, be found in London."

"They say a woman killed him."

"I think so, but it is purely theoretical."

"I dare say; for what motive could any woman have for such a crime?"

"Do you think a woman always requires a motive?" She looked at him in surprise.

"Certainly I do; there can be no cause without an effect."

"In some cases yes," he replied, gravely; "in this case I believe the woman had no motive in committing the crime."

"Then why did she do it?" asked Carmela, looking at him.

"That is what I have to find out," he answered, and so the conversation ended.

It was one o'clock when the steamer got into St. Katherine's

45

Docks, and on the shore crowds of people were waiting to meet their friends. No one, however, came to meet Pat and Ronald, so their mutual sense of loneliness drew them yet closer together.

"Where are you going to stop?" asked Pat, linking his arm in that of the Australian.

"The Tavistock," replied Ronald, "the Australian cricketers generally stop there, so it will feel home-like."

"I'll go there too," sail Ryan promptly, "we'll go to the Alhambra or the Empire to-night, and to-morrow call at the Langham."

"To see whom?"

"Oh a lot of passengers are going to stop there; Miss Lester among the number," said Pat, with a slight blush.

"Oh Pat, your heart is lost there," observed Ronald, smiling.

"And what about your own and the girl from Malta?" asked Pat, whereat Master Ronald also blushed, and the two friends went below to get their stewards to look after their luggage.

Among those who had come on board was a tall elderly gentleman, very straight and severe-looking, scrupulously dresses, with gold-rimmed spectacles, accompanied by a pretty, vivacious-looking brunette, who was clinging to his arm.

"I don't see her Bell," said the gentleman, looking inquiringly round.

"Perhaps she's below papa," said the young lady. "Oh!" with a little scream, "there she is—there she is—Carmela! Carmela!" and with another ejaculation, she ran forward to where Miss Cotoner was standing talking to Vassalla.

"My dear Bell," said Carmela kissing her, "how good of you to come and meet me; how do you do Sir Mark?" and she gave her hand to the elderly gentleman, who now advanced.

"I am pleased to see you looking so well my dear Carmela," he said in cold, measured tones, and then turned an inquiring glance on Vassalla.

"My cousin," said Carmela introducing him; "this is his first visit to England."

Sir Mark and the Marchese both bowed and murmured something, indistinctly.

"We are stopping at the Langham Carmela," said Bell brightly, looking up in Miss Cotoner's face; "papa doesn't like our town house you know, and we're going to stay a fortnight in town! Isn't it Jolly?"

"Bell!" reproved her father, "do not use slang I beg of you."

"I can't help it," said the vivacious Bell, "it was born with me, and—Oh my!" with another little scream, "what a good-looking boy! who is he?"

The quartette turned their heads and saw Ronald, looking

46

handsome and high-bred in his frock coat and tall hat, advancing, evidently with the idea of saying good-bye.

"It's Mr. Monteith," said Carmela, paling a little at the thought that she might not see him again. "You are going away?" she asked, aloud, holding out her hand.

"Yes," he answered, gravely; "Mr. Ryan is with me, and I am going to explore the wilds of London."

"Let me introduce you," said Carmela, despite the black looks of Vassalla; "Sir Mark Trevor, Mr. Monteith; Miss Trevor, Mr. Monteith."

The Australian bowed in his usual grave manner, and then said good-bye to Carmela.

"I shall see you, I presume, in London?" he said, lingering a little.

"If you like to call at the Langham Hotel, I shall be there for a fortnight," she answered, and his face lit up with a happy smile as he went off.

"Why did you do that Carmela?" asked the Marchese in a vexed tone; "we don't want to see him in London."

"You may not; I do," replied Miss Cotoner, with calm contempt. "Shall we go on shore now Sir Mark?" and without another word, she went off with the Baronet and his daughter, leaving him alone.

"So he has not given up the chase yet," muttered Vassalla, as he looked after the luggage, "well, we shall see, we shall see."

Mrs. Pellypop, to her disgust, found no one to meet her, so went off to the Langham Hotel, and wrote a severe letter to the Bishop, which had the effect of bringing the prelate up to London next day.

And so they all went their different ways, and the happy family on board the "Neptune" was scattered abroad through the streets of London town.

Ronald saw the Captain before he left, and had a talk with him about Ventin's death, promising to look up his barrister friend on the morrow. Then he went with Pat to the Tavistock, where they had a capital little dinner, after which they patronised the Alhambra, followed by a supper at the Cavour. Then, though Pat was inclined to make a wet night of it—particularly as they had met several of the boys at the theatre—Ronald went to his hotel, and retired soberly to bed, first, however, posting his letter of introduction to Gerald Foster, of Middle Temple, so that he could call on him on the morrow, and speak with him about the mysterious death of his friend.

"I'll find out who killed poor Ventin," he said as he went to bed, "and then I'll marry Carmela."

47

CHAPTER VIII

COUNSEL'S OPINION

"Everything comes to those who know how to wait." What an excellent proverb for a briefless barrister! Let Mr. Briefless sit in his chambers, surrounded by his law books crammed with learning, and ready to undertake anything—if he wait, will Fame come to him? Not she. Fame is a lazy goddess except when she flies away, and then it is difficult for even the most industrious to catch her and clip her wings.

"He who would seek the wealth of the Indies must take out the wealth of the Indies." Is not that saying a true one? In order to gain fame, riches, and ease, must not one bring industry, perseverance, and knowledge? If Mr. Gerald Foster, barrister, of the Inner Temple, had adopted the motto of knowing how to wait, he might have done so till the end of the chapter, and then have been no better off at the end than the beginning.

But Mr. Foster was not of this fatalistic creed; he did not believe that what must be must, and that if a man is to be famous he will be so whether he idles at home or goes out into the world and works. No; he saw clearly that every day the prizes were fewer and the multitude of competitors greater, and so he did not rest idly on his oars after being admitted to the bar, but went in for hard study, both of men and books. Books, as he knew, are all very well, but according to Pope, the proper study of mankind is man, and Gerald went out into the world and neglected no opportunity of getting fish into his net. He went into the theatrical world, and knew all the most famous actors and actresses in London; he went into the political world, and had all the burning questions of the day at the end of his tongue; he noted the rising and falling of shares on the Stock Exchange, and knew exactly how the money market stood, and he went into society and became acquainted with the follies of the hour.

All this work was for a purpose, for he was a young gentleman who never lost an opportunity, and his sprats were all sent forth to catch mackerel. As yet, in spite of his assiduity to work, and his cultivation of the follies and virtues of his fellow-men, he had succeeded but little, but then he was only twenty-eight years of age, and fortune is not a goddess to be wooed roughly, so he went on, keeping his brain cool, his eyes open, and his mind cultivated, and

48

had no doubt in his own mind that he would succeed. With such indomitable perseverance Gerald knew he must win at last. Fortune, fickle though she he, becomes weary of incessant assaults, and yields in the end to the persevering suitor. So Mr. Gerald Foster, aged twenty-eight, with clever brains, good health, and plenty of tact, worked assiduously at his profession, waiting for the hour that would bring him fame and riches.

Not a handsome man, certainly not; that is, he was not an oiled and curled darling of society. He dressed well, because it was part of his business; but even his kindest friend could not hove pronounced him handsome. A bald head, with a thick fringe of brown hair round it, a prominent nose, a clean-shaven face, with a thin-lipped mouth, and two brilliantly black eyes under bushy eyebrows, he would have been ugly, but for the wonderful charm of his smile. A most delightful smile, that changed all his features, and turned him from the ugly beast into the handsome young prince of the fairy tale. And, above all, his face was one that inspired confidence—an invaluable quality in a lawyer.

On the morning after the arrival of the "Neptune," he sat in his office in the Temple looking over his letters. Accurately dressed, in frock coat, black trousers and tie, and spotless linen, he was turning over his letters, when he came on that of Ronald's, and something in the handwriting of Mr. Monteith senior, seemed to strike him, for he opened it first. Reading it over carefully, he gave vent to a low whistle of astonishment.

"Hum," said Mr. Foster' surveying the letter thoughtfully, "'friend of your father's—only son—first visit to England—would like you to look after him—exactly,'"—laying down the letter—"a cub I expect, with no looks, and less manners, brought up in the wilds, and can't eat his food properly—a delightful aboriginal to introduce into London society. Well, I suppose I must. I love my dear old father too well to think of refusing to do a good turn to any friend of his. Confound it! I'm sure this son is awful. Well, perhaps he'll be rich, and that will cover a multitude of sins. We are fond of whited sepulchres now-a-days."

He put the letter of introduction on one side, and proceeded with the rest of his correspondence, carefully answering each letter, and putting it neatly away. Then he rang for his clerk, and giving him a pile of letters, told him to post them, and taking up the "Daily Telegraph," proceeded to read that paper and wait for clients. Of course, he went first for the money market; then he looked over the political news, glanced at the law reports, and read all the leaders, ending with the theatres. These principal items being finished, he glanced idly over the paper, and at last came on something that interested him.

"Hum," said Mr. Foster, thoughtfully, "a murder committed on board the 'Neptune.' That is the boat the cub came home in. Think I'll read it, that I may have something to talk about when he does come."

He read the article carefully, which told all about Ventin's murder, and the suspicions entertained by Monteith, after which he laid the paper down, and rising from his seat, walked slowly up and down the room with his hands behind his back.

"Don't think the cub can be so bad after all," he said, musingly. "Indeed, judging from his evidence, he seems rather a clever fellow. Queer case, and one I'd like to have a hand in: to unravel a mystery like that would make a fellow's fortune; but these things don't come my way, confound it!"

Here he was interrupted by a knock at the door, and his clerk, a red-headed boy, with a large appetite and fearful dislike for work entered, with a card held in his grimy fingers.

"Gen'lum waitin' sir," said the red-headed youth, who breathed hard in an apoplectic manner. "Ronald Monteith," read Foster on the card; "hum! the cub—show him in Berkles."

Berkles grinned, vanished, and shortly afterwards threw open the door, and announced "Mr. Ronald Monteith."

If ever Gerald Foster got a shock in his life it was seeing the cub of his fancy transformed into the handsome young man of reality. There he stood at the door, hat in hand, tall and noble-looking, quite a distinct being from the ordinary lounger of Regent Street and Hyde Park. Accustomed to rapid observation, Foster took the whole of that stalwart figure and honest countenance in at a glance, and with the sudden liking of instinct advanced towards him with outstretched hand.

"Mr. Monteith I believe?" he said, as Ronald stepped into the room.

"Yes," answered Ronald, grasping the proffered hand—and what an honest firm grip was that of the young Australian; "I sent my letter of introduction to you last night."

"It is here," replied Foster, pointing to the table, as Ronald took his seat.

"I am very glad to see you Mr. Monteith; my father was a great friend of your father's—let us hope the friendship will be hereditary."

"It is very kind of you to say so," said Monteith, in some surprise, "I am quite a stranger to you."

"You are," answered the young lawyer, "but I am a student of

50

Lavater, and I can read faces—therefore, I say, I hope we shall be friends."

"I'm certain we shall," said Ronald, heartily holding out his hand, which the other grasped again.

"You had a pleasant voyage?" asked Foster, in a conversational manner.

"Very, except for one incident."

"Which I know all about,"—pointing to the newspaper.

"I'm glad of that, because, I have just called to see you about it."

"Eh!" said Foster sitting up in his chair; "by Jove, hope you'll put the case in my way. I was just thinking before you came in what a splendid chance was to make a name if one only had the case."

"Well Mr. Foster," said Ronald, slowly, looking keenly at him, "I am very much interested in the case, Ventin was an intimate friend of mine, and as no one that I can hear of is going to try and clear up the mystery of his death, I am going to take that duty on my own shoulders."

"I see," observed Foster nodding sagely; "and you want help?"

"I do—your help."

"You shall have it," cried Foster impulsively; "a subtle case like this is what I require to make my same. At present I am a briefless barrister, but give me the chance and I'm all right. Archimedes wanted a world whereon to rest his lever and move the earth. I am like the Greek. I have the lever—videlicet my brains, now I want a world, namely, a case—this, as far as I can gather from the papers, will be an excellent chance."

"Then you shall have it," said Ronald heartily, "and I am only too glad to think I have such an enthusiastic worker."

"So be it; now tell me the story in your own way; these newspaper accounts are so meagre."

Whereupon Ronald told Foster all about the case, and his own suspicions regarding it, to all of which the young barrister listened carefully, then leaned back in his chair, and put the tips of his fingers together.

"Hum!" he said, thoughtfully, looking up at the ceiling; "you have made out a very strong case against this Maltese wife I must confess; but the evidence is surely circumstantial."

"But who else would have done it?"

"A man might have committed the crime."

"But with what motive?"

"Because he was told to do so."

"But I don't see——"

"Of course you don't," said Foster coolly; "but I will explain, from what you have told me, Mrs. Ventin—we will call her so as we

51

do not know her real name—must have been a woman of very strong passions. Now is it likely that such a woman would remain faithful to her husband? No; I am sure she would not. Depend upon it, she had lovers, or else married again. In the latter case, she might have committed the crime herself, as husbands are not fond of endangering their necks for wives, however pretty; but if she had lovers, depend upon it one of them committed the murder for her sake."

"That's all very well," said Ronald impatiently; "we must not be content with vague speculations but get a clue. Now, how are we to start?"

"I think the idea of Captain Templeton is best," said Foster, thoughtfully, "to look up the divorce case."

"You do not remember it?"

"Not I; there are dozens of divorce cases every year—we are such a moral nation, you know. I can't keep them all in my head; but I will look it up."

"And then?"

"Then I will see the solicitors who had the case in hand, and ask all about Ventin; you knew the man, they knew him, and if your descriptions tally, we will soon establish his identity."

"So far so good," said Ronald, impatiently; "but what follows?"

"Then we must find out where this Maltese wife is——"

"In Malta," said Ronald, abruptly.

"She might not be, by the time we find out her husband's real name," said the barrister coolly; "don't hurry my dear toy; but when we discover where she is, we must set a detective on her to find out her movements on that night when the murder was committed; if she can account for them satisfactorily your theory must fall to the ground."

"But if she can't?"

Foster shrugged his shoulders.

"Then we must be guided by circumstances; we can hardly arrest a woman on the existing evidence; it's a very difficult case, and we must be careful."

"When will you look up this divorce case?"

"To-day, and let you know all about it to-morrow; meanwhile, you had better come and lunch at my club."

"Thank you very much," said Ronald, blushing; "if you will let me away immediately afterwards. I have to make a call."

"Certainly," replied Foster, glancing at his companion's tell-tale face as they went out; "I'll bet he's going to see a woman," he thought, looking at Monteith. "What a transparently honest man he is."

CHAPTER IX

VERSCHOYLE V. VERSCHOYLE
AND MACGREGOR

Business being concluded, as a natural thing, pleasure followed, and having had luncheon with Foster at "The Excelsior," a club much frequented by rising young men, Ronald took leave of the barrister, and went off to his hotel,—there to attire himself for an afternoon call.

It might have been the fashion in the past for lovers to become exceedingly negligent in their dress, and pass their time in writing amatory odes to Chloe and Lydia, not daring to name openly the object of their affections, but now-a-days this is all changed. Strephon puts on his smartest suit, wears his brightest smile, and shows Chloe plainly that he adores her. Instead of wasting his time in writing poetry, he gets Chloe tickets for the theatre, takes her presents of flowers and music, and, on the whole, conducts himself in a matter-of-fact-fashion. So Master Ronald, adopting the modern manner of love-making, dressed himself carefully, placed a flower in his coat, and went off in a hansom cab, to call on Miss Cotoner. He also got a box at one of the theatres and not knowing his divinity's taste in theatricals, judged it by his own, and decided she would like to go to the Frivolity Theatre, at which the sacred lamp of burlesque was burning.

Of course, he found Mr. Ryan there—that young gentleman having come to call on Mrs. Pellypop, and naturally met Miss Lester also—such a delightfully unexpected meeting—the young humbug. It is wonderful how people, who have travelled together, gravitate towards one another on shore, and when Ronald was shown upstairs, he found Mrs. Pellypop, Miss Lester, Carmela and the Marchese, all together having afternoon tea.

Sir Mark and Miss Trevor were also present, and appeared to be enjoying themselves very much. Ronald's entrance was hailed with great delight by all except Vassalla, who scowled at the Australian in a way that showed his animosity had not in any way abated. Carmela came forward with a pretty flush on her cheek, and gave him a cup of tea, after which they all began to talk.

"And what were you doing last night, Mr. Monteith?" asked Mrs. Pellypop, who presided over the tea-service.

53

"Oh!" said Ronald, innocently, not understanding the violent gestures Pat was making to him. "Pat and I went to the Alhambra."

Mrs. Pellypop put down her cup with a look of horror.

"That dreadful place?" she said, looking severely at Pat; "why, Mr. Ryan, you said you were at Exeter Hall."

Everyone laughed at this, and Pat muttered something about a mistake.

"Oh! the Alhambra isn't a bad place," said Sir Mark, good naturedly; "the ballets are very good."

"It's more than the young women are," retorted Mrs. Pellypop, viciously; "I would not like the Bishop to go there."

"No," said Carmela, with a laugh; "it's hardly the place for a bishop."

"I'm sorry you don't like theatres," began Ronald, to the matron, "but——"

"I do like some theatres," answered Mrs. Pellypop; "and any play of Shakespeare's."

"Ah! you see, they aren't playing Shakespeare just now," said Ronald, dryly; "but I've got a box at the Frivolity to-night, and thought the ladies might like to come," looking straight at Carmela.

Everyone looked grave at this. The Frivolity was such a fast theatre.

"You don't know London very well," said Vassalla, in a sarcastic tone of voice, "or you would find out that the Frivolity is as bad, if not worse, than many a music-hall."

"Oh, I've erred through ignorance, then," retorted Ronald, with a flush, "but I don't think music halls are so very bad; and besides, as far as I can judge, your acquaintance with London is not so extensive as to enable you to correct me, Marchese."

Vassalla would have made an angry reply had not Carmela interposed.

"What are they playing there?" she asked.

"A burlesque," cried Kate Lester, "'Artful Artemis and the Shy Shepherd.'"

"Kate," cried Mrs. Pellypop, in a severe tone, "how can you talk so? In my young days girls knew nothing of such things."

"I wish she wouldn't go back into the dark ages," whispered Pat to Carmela, "she must be a hundred, and young at that," whereon Carmela laughed.

"Well," said Ronald, dismally, "if none of the ladies will come, perhaps the gentlemen will."

"I'm engaged," said Vassalla, promptly.

"Thank heaven," thought Ronald, muttering the regrets which politeness demanded.

"I will come, Mr. Monteith," said Sir Mark, "and I've no doubt Mr. Ryan——"

"Oh, I'll be all there," said Pat, gaily; "I adore burlesque; the stage educates the people, begad, and a mighty nice schoolmaster it is."

"That will be three all together," said Ronald, "so I'll ask my friend, Mr. Foster, to make a fourth; but what are the ladies' plans for to-night?"

"I am going to take my cousin and Miss Trevor to the Italian Exhibition," said Vassalla, quickly.

"Not to-night," replied Carmela, coldly, "I am going to write letters."

"And I am going to wait in to see the Bishop," said Mrs. Pellypop.

"In fact," said Bell Trevor, sarcastically, "we are going to have a quiet, domestic evening."

"I hope you'll enjoy yourself," whispered Pat to Miss Lester, as he rose to go.

"Oh, bother," retorted that young lady, crossly; "I might as well be in a convent. The way Mrs. Pellypop looks after me! However, my father is coming to London this week, and then I'll go everywhere."

"May I come too?" plaintively asked Pat.

"If you're good, yes."

As Ronald said good-bye to Carmela, he asked her what she would be doing in the afternoon of the next day.

"Oh! Sir Mark, Miss Trevor, and I are going to the Italian Exhibition."

"And the Marchese?"

"He'll very likely be there also." she replied, coldly.

Whereupon he took his leave, and determined, privately in his own mind, that he also would be at the Exhibition, and would speak to Carmela on the subject nearest his heart.

"I'm madly in love with her," he told Pat, as they went down the street, "you don't know how much."

"Oh, begad I do," retorted Pat, "haven't I got a heart and a girl of my own? I wonder what Lester père is like."

"If he's as nice as Lester fille, it will be all right," laughed Ronald, and they went along to the Temple, as Monteith wanted to introduce Pat to Foster.

This being accomplished, they all went home to dress for dinner, and Sir Mark also turning up, they had a pleasant meal about seven o'clock, and, as all the party suited one another, they became quite jolly. The baronet soon showed himself to be a capital companion; a little cold, perhaps, but with lots of appreciation of fun, and as for Foster, he kept them all amused by his stories and jokes. Pat was in his best form, and the champagne only made him more exuberant in spirits, while Ronald, forgetting all his love and detective work for the moment, was gay as any of them. After dinner they all went to the Frivolity, and arrived just as the curtain was rising on the new burlesque.

The theatre was crowded, as the Frivolity invariably was, and Ronald saw, with some amusement, that the celebrated masher brigade, of whom he had heard so much, was in full force in the stalls. They looked like rows of waxworks with their immovable faces and phlegmatic manners.

"They look as if they ought to be wound up like clockwork," remarked Pat, gaily.

"Oh, they only keep going on tick, if that's what you mean," said Foster, laughing.

"Oh, what a pun!" observed Ronald in disgust; "as if those in the burlesque weren't bad enough."

"Well, they couldn't be much worse," said Sir Mark, putting up his opera glass.

The burlesque of "Artemis" was in the usual style; the author had taken the beautiful Greek myth of Diana and Endymion, and vulgarised it hopelessly. In it, Artemis, the virgin huntress, was represented as an old maid in love with Endymion, who, of course, was in love with some one else, being, in his case, another man's wife, and the other man, being an apothecary, gives Endymion a powder, which sends him to sleep. In fact, the whole burlesque was written to show that women hunt after men, and that the most amusing thing in life is to get as near divorce as possible, without the actual law business taking place. Artemis was acted by a celebrated lion comique, who sang local songs about the Government and the Royal Family, and Endymion was given by a little girl with yellow hair and saucy, blue eyes, who sang and danced like a fairy. Indeed, when she sang her great song, "Slightly on the Mash," Pat fell head over ears in love with her, and felt inclined to join in the chorus with these beautiful words:—

Slightly on the mash, boys,
Don't I do it flash, boys?
Altho' my income's very small,—
In fact, I guess its none at all—
I'll never go to smash, boys,
While I can cut a dash, boys;
For I'm a chap, without a rap
That's—slightly on the mash.

Heavens! how they applauded her as she ogled and flirted, and winked, and smiled; to hear her was a liberal education—in slang.

"Gad, ain't she a jolly little thing," cried Pat, enthusiastically.

"Don't lose your heart, old chap," whispered Ronald, "remember Miss Lester."

"Begad, my heart's big enough for two," said Pat, with a humorous twinkle in his eye; "but ye needn't be afraid, Ronald, I have no diamonds to give away."

"No wonder the theatre elevates the masses," said Gerald to Sir Mark, who was listening to the song with rather a contemptuous smile; "what with burlesques, sensation dramas, aid shilling shockers, we'll soon attain a wonderful degree of civilization."

"Oh! you look at everything from a utilitarian point of view," replied Trevor, as the curtain fell on the first act, amid thunders of applause.

"I try to," began Foster, when Pat, who had caught the last word imperfectly, started up.

"Yes, I'm dry too," he said, gaily; "let us go and worship at the shrine of Bacchus."

"You go with Sir Mark," said Foster; "I want to speak with Monteith on business."

"Right you are!" replied Pat, "come Sir Mark, I'm as thirsty as a limekiln;" and Mr. Ryan went out of the box humming "Slightly on the mash," followed by Sir Mark Trevor, who was greatly amused with the young Irishman.

"Now then," said Ronald, eagerly drawing his chair close to that of Foster's, "what is it, good news?"

"I think so," replied the Barrister, leaning back in his chair, "I fancy I've found out Ventin's real name."

"The deuce you have! and what is it?"

"Leopold Verschoyle."

"Oh! the same initials."

"Exactly, so that accounts for all his linen being marked L. V."

"How did you find out?" asked Ronald.

"After you left me to-day, I went to see a detective called Julian Roper, who is omniscient and knows everyone and everything. I told him the whole affair, and he remembered something about the divorce; I told Mm the time it took place, about six years ago, and we looked up a file of the 'Times' and found out the case, which was not reported at full length, and the information we gained was very scanty. We found out, however, the name of Mrs. Verschoyle's solicitors, and went there—the managing clerk is a great friend of mine, and he let me have the briefs, and they correspond in every particular to the story Ventin, or rather Verschoyle, told you."

57

"Then, you think the identity of Ventin with Verschoyle is fully established?"

"To ourselves, yes—to others no; we have only the bare story told by the deceased to connect him with the case, and the argument against that, is that he might have read about the case in the papers."

"But what motive could he have for telling me such a story?"

"None that I can see—I am only putting a supposititious case; but if we are going in for this, we must get our evidence clear and strong."

"And what is to be done?"

"Come to my chambers to-morrow and see Julian Roper, then we can have a talk over things; we are working completely in the dark at present, but I've no doubt that by to-morrow we shall be in a position to make a start. You have no photograph of the deceased, have you?"

"No; and none were found among his papers, but if I saw one I could tell in a minute if it were Ventin; he was not an ordinary looking man by any means.

"Hum," said Foster, thoughtfully; "that might be managed; if I put Roper to work he'll soon find out a photograph, or," with a sudden idea, "better still, you might look yourself?"

"But where?"

"In some of the big photographers' studios. From what you say, Verschoyle, as we must now call him, must have been a fashionable man, and no one in his position would live thirteen years in London without having had his photograph taken."

"It's a slender chance."

"Very, but you must remember the whole case is a very delicate one."

At this moment Trevor and Pat came in, and immediately afterwards the curtain arose again on a beautiful scene representing Diana's home in the moon, so Foster and Ronald had no more opportunity of talking. Ronald paid no attention to the burlesque, but sat at the back of the box thinking over the whole affair, and the mystery of the case began to pique his curiosity. The other three, however, looked at the stage, admired the pretty girls, encored all the songs, and generally enjoyed themselves. When the curtain fell, Sir Mark invited the whole party to Rule's to supper, and thither they went.

The room upstairs was pretty nearly full, but they succeeded in getting a table to themselves, and ordered supper. The place looked very pretty, with the lights all shaded with green and red shades, and the soft glimmer of the candles shining on the diamonds and bare shoulders of the ladies. Plenty of laughter was going on, varied every now and then by the popping of champagne corks and the clatter of dishes.

"Ain't it a jolly place?" said Pat, looking around with delight, "nice way of winding up the night hullo; Ronald," he went on, "there's our Maltese friend."

And so it was, the Marchese, attired in irreproachable evening costume, was having supper with a young lady beautifully dressed, with a loud voice, and suspicious golden hair. He did not see the others, as he was too busy talking to his friend.

"This is his Italian exhibition, eh?" grinned Pat, who wouldn't have minded changing places with Vassalla.

"Well, perhaps he has been there," said Ronald, carelessly lifting his glass.

"He's brought something good away with him, at all events," replied Ryan; "she's a deuced pretty girl, far too good for Vassalla."

"What name?" asked Foster, with a start.

"Vassalla," interposed Ronald, looking quickly at him.

"Hum, that's odd!"

"What is?"

"I'll tell you all about it to-morrow," was the ambiguous reply.

CHAPTER X

A CONFERENCE OF THREE

Julian Roper was a peculiar character, and had a marked individuality of his own. He was a man of good family, and had been brought up at a public school, the intention of his father being to place him in the army. But Julian objected to his future life being thus mapped out for him, and determined to take his own view of things, and act as inclination led him. This was in the direction of detective work, and his greatest delight was in trying to unravel some mystery of real life which, for strangeness and complication, was far in advance of any work of fiction. But his father, being an aristocratic gentleman of the old school, naturally thought that detective work was not quite the thing for a gentleman, and he sternly commanded his son to dismiss the idea at once. What was the consequence? Julian left his father's house as a prodigal son, and went on the way his particular bias inclined him.

When will fathers learn the great truth that they cannot compel Nature, and that any strong individuality in man or woman is sure to assert itself sooner or later. Every child is not formed on the pattern of its parents, and therefore the parents cannot judge in every case as to the wisdom or fitness of their children's choice. Therefore, as long as the bias is in a right direction, and the children can earn their bread by honourable exercise of their talents, why should they not have free power to display those talents? Julian would have made but an indifferent soldier. As it was, he made an admirable detective, and was noted in London for the quickness of his perception, and the wisdom of his judgments. When the Countess of Darrington's diamonds were stolen, was it not Julian who traced the robbery to none other than the noble lady herself, who had pawned her jewels in order to pay her lover's debts?

When Michael Cantwell was charged with poisoning his wife, was it not Roper who discovered that the wife had poisoned herself, and left a letter laying the blame on her husband out of revenge? Why, these stories are the common talk of the detective force, and when Gerald Foster asked Roper to take the "Verschoyle Mystery" in hand, he knew he had got a good man, with the sagacity of a sleuth-hound, and the inflexible determination of a Richelieu.

And, indeed, when the case was explained to Julian by the barrister, that astute gentleman had eagerly agreed to do his best in

60

discovering the culprit, for it was a mystery which delighted his soul. In fact, Roper was in love with these Chinese puzzles of social life, and nothing pleased him so much as spending months in adding, link by link, to a chain of evidence ending, in the complete clearing up of a curious case.

So the three gentlemen sat in Foster's office, and talked the case over. Ronald; eager and attentive to the views of the others; Foster, quiet, cynical, and keen; and Roper, calm and unfathomable, with his sharp, blue eyes bent on both, and his acute hearing taking in every word said.

It is no use sketching Roper's portrait, for like Proteus he had many shapes, and what the real Roper was no one knew. One day he would be a parson, the next, a sporting gentleman, the third day a tramp, and so on, until the noble fraternity of thieves actually began to suspect each other, so ubiquitous and clever was the famous detective.

"It's the strangest case I was ever in," said Mr. Roper, in his soft, low voice; "but one which it will be a pleasure to work at. At present we have the merest clue. Now, the great thing is to follow it up."

"First," said Foster, taking some papers from the drawer of his desk, "let us look at the divorce case, 'Verschoyle v. Verschoyle and Macgregor.'"

"Oh, we know all about that!" said Ronald, impatiently.

"Not all of it," replied Gerald, smoothing the brief. "In the first place what do you think was the name of Mrs. Verschoyle?"

"Her maiden name?"

"Yes."

"I don't know."

"Then I will tell you. Cotoner!"

"What?"

Ronald sprang to his feet as pale as death.

"Yes," said Julian Roper, pulling out his pocket-book; "did not a lady of that name come on board the 'Neptune' at Malta?"

"My God!" cried Ronald, madly, "you don't mean to say——"

"We mean to say nothing," answered Foster, quietly; "except that the young lady you know is innocent of this crime."

Ronald gave a kind of strangled sob.

"It is sacrilege even to think of her in connection with it!" he said, in a stifled voice; his young face now haggard with pain. "Why, the Maltese wife was thirty, and Miss Cotoner is only twenty-six! Vassalla, her cousin, was with her all the time she was on board before the ship started. She had no motive for killing Verschoyle. She didn't even know him when I spoke about him."

61

"Not as Verschoyle, no," from Roper.

"Do you believe this?" asked Ronald, savagely.

"No, I don't," replied the detective, blandly; "but we may as well look at all sides of the question. I daresay Miss Cotoner is as innocent as you or I of this crime. Still, we must lose no opportunity of getting evidence."

"Stop a moment," said Ronald, calmly; "because the name of Mrs. Verschoyle was Cotoner I do not see that Miss Cotoner is implicated—there are, no doubt, more people than one of that name in Valletta."

"Of course there are," said Foster, quietly; "but Miss Cotoner's mother's maiden name was Vassalla."

"What?"

"Yes! that was the reason of my surprise, when I heard the name last night."

"That proves nothing."

"Only that her cousin's name is also Vassalla. So it proves, pretty clearly, that Miss Cotoner is Mrs. Verschoyle's sister."

Ronald groaned; for there flashed across him Verschoyle's remark that his wife had Arab blood in her veins, and that Miss Cotoner had made the same statement at Gibraltar; so it seemed true, after all.

"Go on," he said, huskily; "what is to be done now?"

"The best thing to be done," said Roper, quietly, "is to find out some one who knew Verschoyle."

"Yes, but how can you find out such a person?"

"I have done so!"

"Already?"

"Yes; he has a sister staying in London, and I know where to find her."

"Indeed."

"Yes; she is a Mrs. Taunton, and her husband is at artist; if we could see her and get her to show Mr. Monteith a portrait of the deceased, he would be able to recognise it."

"Of course I should," said Ronald, eagerly.

"Then," pursued Mr. Roper, without altering his voice; "there is another bit of evidence we must get hold of; the letter sent by the wife to Verschoyle, saying she would kill him."

"But how can we obtain that?"

"Well," shrugging his shoulders, "I am going on a forlorn hope. Mrs. Taunton may have it."

"Nonsense," said Foster, incredulously.

"I dare say it is—but still there is a chance that Verschoyle, when going to Australia, left some of his papers behind; a man does not care about dragging a lot of luggage all over the world, and it is very likely that Mrs. Taunton has some of her brother's things to look after, till he returned."

"And if this paper is among the things?"

"In that case," observed the detective; "we must get some writing of Mrs. Verschoyle, and compare the two; if they correspond, we shall have strong evidence that she is the criminal."

"And then?"

"Then I will go out to Malta, and see if I can ascertain her movements on the night in question. By the way," to Ronald, "what date was it you left Malta?"

"I think it was the 13th of June."

"Thank you," replied Roper, noting it in his pocket-book; "then I want to find out where she was on the 13th of June between seven and nine o'clock p.m."

"But instead of you going to Malta, why couldn't Monteith ask Miss Cotoner?"

"I won't," burst out Ronald, savagely; "what has she to do with it—she isn't the wife."

"No, but she might be the wife's sister."

Ronald thought a moment.

"Yes, she might," he answered, pale as death; "but all the same, you haven't proved that yet, and I won't insult her by asking her."

Roper sighed as he looked at this stubborn young man; it was no good trying to get assistance from him, so he would have to do the best he could.

"Very well," he said, calmly; "we won't ask Miss Cotoner anything. The first thing to be done is to establish the identity of Ventin with Verschoyle, and then I will go to Malta and see about Mrs. Verschoyle."

"But, how are we to find Mrs. Taunton?" asked Foster.

"There is a meeting of the 'Society for the Improvement of Art,' to-night," said Roper, "and she is sure to be there with her husband."

"Oh, I've got tickets," said Gerald; "so myself and Monteith will go, and we'll soon find out all about her and her brother; will you come, Monteith?"

"No," doggedly.

"Why not?"

"Because I don't want to go on with this case any more."

"I can understand your reason," said Roper; "you think Miss Cotoner may be mixed up in it."

"No, I don't."

"Yes, you do, sir—apologising for the contradiction; but if you want to find out who killed Verschoyle, you had better go on with the case; it will be more satisfactory to yourself and"—hesitating—"Miss Cotoner."

"She has nothing to do with it."

"Of course not," said Roper, soothingly; "we've only the similarity of name to go by. I think I would go to this meeting to-night sir, if I were you."

Ronald thought a moment——"Very well, I will," he said resignedly; and then Roper arose to take his leave.

"I'll look in to-morrow, and see what information you've obtained," he said. "Good-day, Mr. Foster—good-day, Mr. Monteith."

"Good-day," replied Ronald, not taking his eyes off the table.

Julian and Foster went out.

"Is he in love with her?" asked the detective.

"He is!"

"I thought so; this case will be harder than you or I think."

"But you don't suppose Miss Cotoner had anything to do with it?"

"No; but I think she's the sister of the woman who committed the crime."

CHAPTER XI

AN ARTISTIC EVENING

"The Society for the Improvement of Art" was one of the favourite fads of the day, and will no doubt hold its own till some newer "fad" comes to the front, and then it will fall to pieces. It was organized by three or four enthusiasts, who said there was a great deal of latent artistic talent in England which needed development, and they proposed to let everybody, who thought he or she could draw, have an exhibition once a year. Every picture sent in was hung on the walls of their saloon, and some queer things figured there. Unappreciated geniuses with the talents, as they thought, of Michael Angelo, sent in hideous productions, which were enough to send a painter of any knowledge whatever crazy, such was the crudity of the drawing. Some of the pictures were done in a firm, precise manner, as if they were the productions of very young people, and finished by the Governess; others had a dashing, sketchy appearance, as if they had been done in half an-hour, a not unlikely thing; but here and there were some really pretty sketches that were admired. Yet the whole effect of these walls, disfigured in such a manner, was depressing in the extreme. The fact was, the Society for the Improvement of Art was a collection of amiable idiots, who made their mad project an excuse for having evenings when everybody who was anybody went.

On this evening, therefore, the rooms were crowded with all sorts of queer people; some who thought themselves clever, but were not, and tried to make up for their lack of brains by assuming extraordinary costumes; others, who were dressed in the height of fashion only came because everyone else was there; and critics, actors, artists, and literary men all jostled one another in the crowd, and laughed to scorn the feeble efforts of the Society to find hidden talent. There was weak tea, and thin bread-and-butter, and everybody, when they were not looking at the pictures—which was seldom—talked scandal and abused their friends, so it was all very delightful and amusing.

At least Monteith found it so, as he leaned against the wall, and listened to Foster's cynical comments on all who passed along, mostly friends of his own; but, after all, what is the use of having friends if one can't abuse them?

"You see that bald-headed old chap there?" said Signor

Asmodeus Foster, who was about to unroof his friends' houses for the benefit of the Australian, "the one with the gaunt female beside him—she was his daughter's governess, and married him by force; she bullies the life out of him, and if he but look at another woman—a thing, by the way, the old scamp is very fond of doing—he catches it when he gets home. That pretty little woman in white is Lady Aspasia, who was not as good as she might be—once—but now she's married and gives good dinners, so Society doesn't rake up her little failures in the past. We are a very generous people when there's money in the question. That young dandy, with the simper and the eye-glass, is Bertie Hardup, who a year ago had not a shilling—his face was his fortune, and a mighty nice income it brought him, for he married Miss McNab, the Scotch heiress, who has red hair and a long pedigree; he doesn't care a fig about her, and keeps Musidora, of the Frivolity, out of McNab's money. By Jove, my dear fellow, all these people have their skeletons, and if they could only become visible, you'd see every one of them attended by a bony figure like those in the Dance of Death."

"Rather a ghastly assemblage," said Ronald, absently.

"Not at all," replied his companion; "bless you, we love our skeletons, and, in the middle of the night, take them out and discuss our private affairs with them; then we lock them up in the little dark cupboards again, and only hear the faint rattle of their bones during the day."

Ronald laughed.

"You are cynical!"

"The fault of the world my dear boy. I would like to go through life keeping all my youthful illusions, but the world won t let me—it has destroyed all my dreams of honour and honesty one by one till—pouf!—it has made me as disbelieving as St. Thomas."

"What strange people are here," said Ronald, looking at the restless crowd.

"Yes!—the dresses are eccentric, are they not?—but that is part of our trade in London; if one cannot be famous—well, the greatest idiot can make himself conspicuous. Let us walk through the rooms to find Mrs. Taunton, or we'll miss her."

Ronald, nothing loth, went off with his Mentor, and could not help laughing at the curiously dressed people he saw. One lady was arrayed in black velvet, trimmed with silver, and looked like a first-class coffin; while another in white, with large red rosettes down the front of her dress, had such square shoulders that she resembled nothing so much as a chest of drawers. Here and there were some pretty girls, but the general impression Ronald had was disappointment at the appearance of the ladies.

66

"They're so deucedly ugly," he said in disgust.

"Yes, they can't make their faces up properly," observed Foster, putting on his eye-glass; "they're all like very badly painted pictures—but that's a pretty woman over there."

"Yes, by gad, she is," replied Ronald critically; "who is she?"

"The lady we are in search of—Mrs. Taunton—come, and I'll introduce you to her."

So Foster, followed by Ronald, pushed his way through the crowd towards Mrs. Taunton, who was standing with her husband, a tall round-shouldered man to whom she was talking in a vivacious manner. A very charming lady she was—small, fair-haired, and wonderfully bright and quick in her conversation and actions. Her face was wreathed with smiles, but during a pause in the conversation it was in repose for a moment, and then Ronald detected a shade of latent melancholy which reminded him somewhat of the sombre expression of his dead friend's face.

"How do you do, Mrs. Taunton?" said Foster, when he reached her side; "I have not seen you for at least—let me see—a hundred years!"

"If that is the case," replied the little lady, laughing, "you must have the gift of immortality, for you don't look a day older."

"Nor you a minute," said Foster, with a bow. "Permit me to introduce to you my friend, Mr. Monteith; he is come from the wilds of Australia to see if civilization is an improvement on savagery."

"Welcome to London, Mr. Monteith," said Mrs. Taunton, putting out her hand with a sunny smile; "I hope we shall be able to make your stay pleasant."

"I'm sure of that," answered Ronald, heartily, "in such company it would be foolish not to enjoy myself."

"What! they know how to make compliments in Australia?"

"When they have a worthy object," with a bow.

"Another! really, Mr. Monteith, you are a Sir Charles Grandison.'

"I hope not," broke in Foster, who had been talking to Mr. Taunton; "he was a prig,—wouldn't be tolerated now-a-days; but then," shrugging his shoulders, "how could you expect a linen-draper to conceive a gentleman? It would be easier to make a silk purse out a sow's ear."

"Poor Richardson," said the lady, with an amused look, "how severe you are on him. Mr. Monteith, pardon my rudeness; let me introduce to you my husband."

The artist bowed, and shook Ronald by the hand, but said nothing. He was a man of few words, and so left his wife to do most of the talking—a task to which she was fully equal.

"Now then," said Mrs. Taunton, when the introduction had been effected, "Mr. Foster, you can talk art, law, and scandal to my husband, while Mr. Monteith escorts me through the room in order to improve his mind."

Ronald, of course, was delighted, and they strolled off, leaving the lawyer in deep conversation with the artist over a divorce case which was then being published in extenso in the newspapers.

What charming conversationalists some women are! They are as happy in their talk as in their letter-writing; and Mrs. Taunton was a most delightful cicerone; with all Foster's knowledge and wit, but without his cynicism. Cynicism, like garlic, should only be used in moderation, and Ronald found Mrs. Taunton's bright, rapid talk rather a relief after the pessimistic views of his friend, the lawyer. The lady seemed to know everyone—stopped every now and then to talk to people, and, after leaving them, kept up a running fire of conversation about their oddities, which amused the Australian very much.

"How you do seize on people's weak points!" he said, laughing.

"Of course," she replied, "I'm a woman, and have the instinct of the sex."

"Likewise the charms."

"Mr. Monteith, I cannot allow you to pay me any more compliments to-night; but you may call to-morrow at four, if you like, and I shall be prepared for your gallantry."

"I should like it above all things," he said, seriously.

"Why, how grave your face is! I shall have to call you the knight of the rueful countenance. Is anything the matter?"

"I don't know; there might be."

"What an ambiguous reply!" she said, glancing at him curiously. "Are you a spiritualist? Have you had an intimation that all is not right in the other worlds?"

Her flippancy displeased him, knowing the importance of the matter in question.

"Mrs. Taunton," he said, gravely, looking down at the little figure from his tall height, "I was introduced to you for a purpose, and I am going to take a liberty."

Mrs. Taunton looked a little frightened, and wondered if her good-looking cavalier were mad. He guessed her thoughts.

"Don't be afraid, I am in my senses,"

"Then he must be in love with me," thought Mrs. Taunton, in dismay at this eccentric young man; but his next remark caused her to alter her mind.

"You have a brother?" he said, abruptly.

"Yes," she replied, rather puzzled, "I have one brother. I think

68

he is out in Australia. Why," a sudden light breaking in on her, "have you met him?"

"I think so."

"What is he doing?" she asked, eagerly.

Ronald parried the question.

"I don't know," he replied; "but I'll tell you all about him to-morrow."

"Is he ill, or in trouble?" she said, quickly. "Please tell me, because I am very—very fond of him."

"Mrs. Taunton," he said, quietly, "I am come here for a purpose."

"Which concerns my brother?"

"Yes. Believe me, I do not ask out of idle curiosity, but will you answer my questions?"

Mrs. Taunton thought a moment.

"It's all so curious," she said, nervously, "but Mr. Foster, who introduced you, is an old friend of mine,"—after a pause, "yes, I will answer your questions."

He led her to a seat and took one beside her, then began to talk.

"Your brother's name is Leopold Verschoyle?"

"Yes."

"He was married in Malta seven years ago?"

"He was."

"And a year afterwards separated from his wife?"

"He did."

"And then?" hesitatingly.

"Oh, do not be afraid," she said, coldly; "he fell in love with another woman, and there was a divorce case."

"Verschoyle v. Verschoyle and Macgregor."

"You seem to know all about it," replied the lady, a little astonished. "He went to Australia with Miss Macgregor, and since then I have heard nothing about him. What became of them?"

"He married her."

"Oh!" drawing down the corners of her mouth, "then she is his wife now I presume?"

"No; she is dead!"

"Dead! Then my brother is coming back to England?"

"That I cannot tell you till I call on you, to-morrow."

"What do you want me to do?"

"To show me your brother's portrait—have you one?"

"Yes; only one. Taken just before he left for Malta."

"Good. Then I will call to-morrow at four o'clock."

"And then?" rising and taking Monteith's arm.

"I will tell you everything," he replied.

"About what?"

"That depends on—to-morrow."

"You are a most mysterious man," said Mrs. Taunton, in a vexed tone, as he took her back to her husband; "you arouse my curiosity, and then refuse to gratify it—but tell me at least one thing—is my brother well?"

Ronald hesitated. He dare not tell her that her brother—if Ventin indeed, were her brother—was dead so he equivocated.

"I think so," he replied, hurriedly.

"Then I will wait for your promised revelation to-morrow;" and, with a smile, she left him, and went back to her husband, who was still talking to Foster.

"Take me home, George," said Mrs. Taunton, touching her husband's arm; "I am tired."

"Yes, you look pale, my dear," he answered, giving her his arm; "we'd better go at once."

Foster glanced keenly at her and then at Ronald, who, however, shook his head.

"Good night, Mr. Foster," said Mrs. Taunton, giving him her hand; "you are to call on me to-morrow at four, with Mr. Monteith?"

"I will not fail," he replied, with a smile; and taking her husband's arm she moved away, and was soon lost among the crowd.

When she disappeared, Gerald turned to the Australian, quickly.

"Well?"

"I asked her about her brother," said Monteith, quietly; "and her story corresponds in every particular with that of Ventin."

"Then you think Verschoyle is Ventin?"

"Yes, I think so; but I will be certain to-morrow."

"Oh! in what way?"

"Mrs. Taunton is going to show me her brother's portrait."

"And then?"

"Well," observed Monteith, "if it is Ventin as I suspect, I think it will be the beginning of the end."

CHAPTER XII

THE MISSING LINK

What queer old places there are in Brocade Street—why, the very name is suggestive of the stately times of the early Georges, and indeed, Brocade Street was a fashionable locality even earlier, when Queen Anne was ruling, and Marlborough was winning his brilliant victories, and Duchess Sarah was alternately bullying and coaxing her weak-minded mistress. A dark, narrow street with tall houses of red brick on either side, innumerable windows, and heavy-looking doors which had often opened to let out Belinda to her sedan-chair, or Sir Plume on the way to Wills, to have a chat with Sterne and Addison.

Fancy Swift, with his dark, lowering face, walking down this street with his thoughts fixed upon a possible bishopric, or Dick Steele, swaggering along in his rich dress, stopping to take off his hat to Lady Betty Modish, who looked archly at him through the window. And then, at night, when all the streets were in darkness, save for the link boys, poor lost Richard Savage wandering about in company with Samuel Johnson even at that early age burly and contradictory. Ah, yes; great spirits were abroad in those stirring times, and Brocade Street could tell a few stories of interest, had it a voice; but now the tide of fashion had rolled westward, and the street was left silent and lonely to think over its past glories.

All those famous old houses, with their broad, oak staircases and large, stately apartments, were now used as lodging-houses for decayed gentlefolk; and city clerks found shelter in the rooms which had once re-echoed to the brilliant epigrams of Swift, or the smooth utterances of Joseph Addison.

There were also some artists to be found in the street, for they loved it for its old associations and the dead-world flavour which haunted all the houses?-a perfume of past memories of the beaux and belles of Good Queen Anne's gay Court.

Among these was Mr. Taunton, who occupied a tall, gaunt, grim-looking mansion at the upper end, and, though his merry little wife tried hard to persuade him to move to a more civilized locality, he steadily refused to exchange the dead glories of Brocade Street for the fashionable quarters of Kensington. So, Mrs. Taunton did the best she could, and beautified the quaint, oak-panelled rooms with rich tapestries, curious old china, and bizarre-looking brasses.

She sat now in her drawing-room waiting for Mr. Monteith and his friend, and wondering what could be the reason of their visit. The soft light of the day somewhat subdued by the long curtains which draped the windows, stole into the room and all the picturesque objects were seen in a kind of semi-twilight. Here, a tall column with the bust of a laughing Menade in marble, looking white and still against a background of crimson plush, and there, a landscape picture on an easel with some silken drapery flung carelessly over it. Plenty of easy chairs, spindle-legged tables of Chippendale, cupboards of priceless china, great jars from the Flowery Land which could have hidden the Forty Thieves, and innumerable mirrors all over the walls interspersed with pictures both in oil and watercolours.

Mrs. Taunton herself, in a tea-gown of some soft, clinging material, was flitting about here and there like a restless butterfly— now arranging some flowers with deft hands, and again touching the dainty tea-service of Sèvres china which stood at the end of the room.

"I do wish those men would be punctual," said Mrs. Taunton, for the tenth time, as she stood at one of the long windows and looked down the dismal street; "I feel so miserable being alone."

Her husband was up in his studio painting, so she sat down on the window seat, and leaning her head on her hand began to soliloquize.

"I wonder what that Mr. Monteith wants to tell me," she said to herself; "he must have some news of Leopold; I'm sure I hope so; it is years since I heard from him; and then he left such a lot of things with me; all those jewels which belonged to mother. I hope there's nothing wrong, but I dare say it's all right; Leopold could always look after himself. Ah!" as the rattle of wheels was heard, "there they are," and she left the window quickly, as a hansom drove up to the door.

In a few moments Mr. Monteith and Mr. Foster were announced, and Mrs. Taunton received them with a face wreathed in smiles far different from the melancholy countenance which had gazed out of the window a few moments since. A wonderfully pretty woman she looked in her pale, yellow tea-gown as she advanced to greet the young men with the polished charm of a thorough woman of the world.

"It's rather chilly to-day," observed Monteith, when they were all comfortably seated, and Mrs. Taunton was busy at the tea-table.

"Chilly!" echoed Mrs. Taunton. "Oh! you don't know what cold weather is in London. Wait till you see a fog, a nice, thick, yellow

72

fog, with the sun like a ball of red fire glaring thro' it, then you'll say its chilly."

"Ugh," said the Australian, with a shudder, "your description is suggestive of the charnel-house."

"Monteith longs for the blue skies of Australia," said Foster, with a laugh, as he received his cup of tea from his hostess.

"So would you," retorted Ronald, "if you had once been there. Life in Australia is like the prairie fever, one is always longing to be back again."

"Perhaps that's the reason my brother stops out there so persistently?" said Mrs. Taunton, leaning back in her chair.

The two gentlemen suddenly became grave, whereat the lady sat up again.

"What do you mean by all this mystery," she asked impetuously; "last night Mr. Monteith roused my curiosity to the highest pitch about my brother, and then refused to gratify it. Is anything wrong? Has Leopold run away with another man's wife, or found a gold mine, or committed a murder, or what?"

She tried to speak lightly, but there was a ring of anxiety in her tones.

"You promised to show me his portrait," said Monteith, suddenly looking up.

Mrs. Taunton arose without a word, and going to a distant table, took up a photograph framed in purple plush, which she placed in Monteith's hands.

"Taken seven years ago," she said.

Monteith looked at the dark, handsome face of the portrait with a vague expression of sadness in his eyes, and handed it to Foster with a sigh:—

"It is Lionel Ventin."

"Ah!" said Foster, with a long breath, as he looked at it, "I thought as much."

"What do you mean by calling my brother Lionel Ventin?" asked Mrs. Taunton quickly, clasping her hands; "that is—that is the name of the man that was—that was—murdered!" The last word came out almost in a shriek as she sprang to her feet.

Monteith nodded sadly.

"Yes," he replied, gravely, "Leopold Verschoyle and Lionel Ventin are the same."

"Then he—my brother is the man who was murdered on board the Neptune?" she asked, in a whisper.

Foster arose in alarm.

"Let me get you some water," he said, advancing towards her, but she waved him back.

73

"Was my brother the man?"

Monteith bowed.

"And you gave evidence at the inquest?"

He bowed again.

Mrs. Taunton braced herself up with a mighty effort, her charming face looking pale, and drawn with horror. She walked away a few steps, then suddenly wheeled round on the two men, who were watching her silently:—

"Who killed him?"

"That is what we intend to find out," said Monteith, slowly, "and you must assist us."

Mrs. Taunton sat down, and, clasping her hands over her knee, sat staring at the Australian with a rigid face. The shadows were falling fast in the street outside, and through the gathering gloom of the room the two men could see the white, set face of this woman looking like that of a lost spirit.

"Do you know what grief is?" she asked, in a dull, hard voice; "do you know what it is to go about with a smile on your lips, and a broken heart? No, of course you don't—you are men; and cannot feel pain as a woman can. I have lost two children, and it nearly broke my heart—my husband is wrapped up in his work, and does not care for me except as a useful ornament to his table—the only two children I had died when I most wanted their love and affection, and I thought my heart would break—perhaps it did—but—I lived—yes—I went about with a smiling face, and talked gaily with my friends—they said I was heartless. God! If they only knew the nights of agony that succeeded to days of apparent joy—but I lived—yes, and I still go about amusing myself—a maelstrom above, but a hell below. This is another blow. I loved my brother dearly, though I had not seen him for years, and now he is dead—murdered—by whom?—you do not know—I do!"

"What do you mean?" asked Monteith, starting to his feet.

She sprang forward and caught his wrist.

"Did he not tell you the story of his life—how he was ruined by a woman?"

"Elsie Macgregor?"

"No, she tried to save him; it is not her I mean—you know—his wife—his Maltese wife, Bianca Cotoner."

Monteith fell back in his chair, and covered his face with his hands. Heavens, was it all true then? was the girl he loved the sister of a murderess? And yet, though it looked so black against her, where was the proof? He looked up suddenly.

"There is no proof," he began.

74

"Proof!" she flashed out, quickly; "you want proof—I can supply it." And she ran quickly out of the room.

"What does she mean?" asked Monteith.

"I know," said Foster, sagaciously; "she has gone for that paper."

"Impossible!"

"I don't see what other proof she can have," said the barrister, shrugging his shoulders.

"It's impossible—it's impossible, I tell you," cried Monteith, vehemently; "his wife might have killed him, but she was not a Miss Cotoner."

"The evidence both of the Divorce Court and Mrs. Taunton says she was."

"But she cannot be the sister of Carmela."

"I cannot say there may be more Cotoner families than one in Malta; but still, Vassalla's name being mixed up in it seems to point out that she might be."

"I won't believe it till I hear the truth from her own lips."

"You will ask her, then?"

"No!"

"That's a mistake; you'll only torture yourself till you get a satisfactory explanation."

Monteith flung himself back in his chair with a low moan, his bright young face looking pinched and haggard in the dim light, and at this moment Mrs. Taunton entered the room, carrying a desk in her hands.

"This is my brother's," she said, placing it on a table, and turning to the young men. "He sent it to me about a year ago, and asked me to keep it for him, as he was going to South America, and did not want to take it with him. He also sent the key, and I looked over the contents; they are principally letters."

She flung back the lid of the box, and there were bundles of letters, yellow with age, tied up with red tape. There was also a portrait—a faded old portrait of a girl's face.

"Is this the Maltese wife?" asked Foster, taking it up, whereon Monteith sprang to his feet, and also looked to see if it resembled Carmela.

Mrs. Taunton made a gesture of dissent.

"It is Elsie Macgregor."

The young man looked curiously at that face—a quiet, patient face, with love and truth shining through the pure eyes—the face of the woman that had ruined her life to save Leopold Verschoyle from himself. Foster laid it reverently down again amongst the old letters.

75

"She was a good woman," he said, softly, and cynic as he was, he meant it.

"But the proof—the proof!" said Monteith, impatiently.

Mrs. Taunton rapidly turned over the bundles of letters, and drew from one packet a square slip of yellowish paper, which she handed to Monteith in silence. He took it eagerly, and read the contents—only three lines:

"You have treated me shamefully, and I will never forgive you for it. We women of the South can revenge ourselves, and your life will pay the penalty of your falseness."

There was no signature or date to this extraordinary document, and the two men wondered at it for a minute, then Foster looked up suddenly.

"How do you know this is from the wife?" he asked, sharply.

Mrs. Taunton pointed to the letters.

"Of course, I have not read them," she said, coldly; "but you will see the writing on the envelopes corresponds with that in the letter."

And so it did, in every particular; so Monteith and Foster both came to the conclusion that this wife must have killed Verschoyle, seeing that she had threatened him thus, and the crime was committed at Malta, where she lived—the proofs were so clear.

"What are you going to do?" asked Mrs. Taunton, impatiently.

"I have a detective in my employment, called Julian Roper," said Monteith, slowly; "and if you give me this paper, I will show it to him—then he must go out to Valletta—find out where Mrs. Verschoyle lives, and ascertain her movements on the night the crime was committed."

"And he must also get some of her writing, to see if it corresponds with this," said Foster, pointing to the paper.

"When will he start?" asked Mrs. Taunton, quickly.

"To-morrow, by a P. and O. steamer," said Monteith; "and we will hear all particulars from him in a fortnight."

"Very well," replied Mrs. Taunton, quietly; "you can take the paper, and hunt that woman down, for she and none other killed my poor brother—good-bye, gentlemen, I am going to lie down;" and without another word, she left the room, and retired to her bedroom, where her overtaxed nerves gave way, and she broke down utterly.

"She is a plucky woman, that," said Foster, as they left the house, and drove away; "what do you think of it all?"

"I think," said Monteith, thoughtfully, "that the case looks very black against the former Mrs. Verschoyle, but what I want to be certain of is her relationship to Carmela."

"You can find out by asking her."

"No, I will not," said the Australian, doggedly; "but Roper can find out in Valletta, and if it turn out to be so, I'll speak to Carmela about the crime, and see what she knows."

"Suppose she prove the sister, Mrs. Verschoyle, a murderess, will you give up Carmela?"

"No," he answered, curtly. "I don't see why the sins of the father should be visited on the children, nor that one woman should be punished for the crime of another."

CHAPTER XIII

THE APPLE OF DISCORD

Altogether Foster was very pleased with the position of affairs, as there was now some tangible evidence to go upon. In the first place it had been satisfactorily ascertained that Lionel Ventin was identical with Leopold Verschoyle, and in the second the handwriting of the wife of the deceased showed that she deliberately intended to commit the crime, and to all appearances had achieved her object while the steamer was lying at Malta.

"The next thing to be done," said Foster to Ronald and Roper as they sat in his room, "is to obtain evidence as to Mrs. Verschoyle's movements on that night. Now, my impression is that she came on board to see her sister off to England, and while there, saw her husband, heard him tell you the number of his cabin—followed him, and after committing the crime, mixed in the crowd, and returned on shore undetected."

"A very feasible theory," retorted Ronald, in a vexed tone; "but you forget—you have yet to prove that Miss Cotoner is Mrs. Verschoyle's sister.

"That can be at once settled by asking Miss Cotoner."

Ronald moved uneasily in his seat.

"I suppose it must come to that," he replied; "but before asking her, I think it best that Roper should go to Malta, and find out all about Mrs. Verschoyle."

"I can go to-morrow," said Roper, promptly, "and as soon as I find out what you want to know, I'll write at once."

So it was settled. Julian Roper went out to Malta the next day, and there was nothing left for Monteith to do but to wait and see what evidence could be found against Mrs. Verschoyle. He felt very miserable over the whole affair, and particularly as it seemed probable that Carmela would be mixed up in it, and then—well, he did not like to dwell on the thought of such a possibility.

And Carmela?

She, on her part, was quite as unhappy as her lover, because she could not understand his changed attitude towards herself. Formerly he had been assiduous in his attendance on her, but now he rarely came near her, and was always making excuses regarding his absence, excuses which she plainly saw were feigned and forced. She was too proud, however, to complain, and went about as usual with Sir Mark and his daughter—frequented balls, theatres, garden parties, picture galleries, and all the sights of London, never once showing how deeply she felt Ronald's desertion.

Cold, stately, and self-possessed as of old, a keen eye might yet have noticed the dark circles under her eyes, and the increasing pallor of her face. Bell noticed it, and told her father, who, becoming alarmed, wanted to take Carmela down to Marlow at once.

"These London gaieties are too much for you, my dear," he said, anxiously; "you are not used to late hours."

"Oh, I am quite well," answered Carmela, with assumed gaiety; "it is only a little fatigue; you must not hurry me away just when I am enjoying myself."

"Fancy calling this sort of thing enjoyment!" said Bell, contemptuously; "I'm sick of these miles of streets, and crowded dances, and conceited men; give me the country, with a bright sky and a good horse."

"We'll go down soon, then," said Carmela, kissing her; "I only want to stay in town another week, and then I shall be at your disposal."

The fact was, Carmela was cherishing a hope that Ronald would see her, and explain away the discord which seemed to have arisen between them. But though he called occasionally he made no sign, but retained the same reserved demeanour, the reason of which she could not guess.

Ronald, as a matter of fact, was torturing himself over the position of affairs. Was Carmela the sister of Mrs. Verschoyle? If so, she must have been in love with Verschoyle, as his dead friend had clearly said so. In this case he—Ronald—was not her first love, and he felt that such a position was very unsatisfactory.

Another thing was, if Carmela had been standing beside her sister on the night of departure, she also must have recognized Verschoyle, and therefore, when the murder was committed, she must undoubtedly have connected her sister with the crime. And suppose she knew all about it, and was silent in order to shield her sister. Well, he could not blame her for that; but if she were doing this, she was, in a certain way, an accomplice: and could he marry a woman who was not only cognizant of such a crime, but was closely related to the person who had committed it?

Ronald used to lie awake at night, and worry over these things till he thought he should go out of his mind. He was madly in love with Carmela, but still he had a certain amount of self-restraint, and determined not to ask her to be his wife until the mystery which environed the death of Verschoyle was cleared up satisfactorily. Therefore he kept away from her, as he dared not trust himself in her presence without giving way and marrying her without taking anything into consideration.

And so these two young people were in a singularly unhappy position—both in love, yet both living at cross purposes; Carmela wondering at Ronald's sudden change of demeanour, and Ronald trying to solve the doubts which had arisen in his mind concerning the woman he loved.

As to the rest of the "Neptune's" passengers, they were scattered far and wide. Pat Ryan had gone off to look after his Irish estates, which mainly consisted of acres of bog inhabited by evil-minded tenants, who refused to pay the rent, and as Pat was too kind-hearted to evict them, his income was growing beautifully less every day. Kate Lester and her mother had gone down to Hampshire, on a visit to a rich bachelor uncle, who had fallen in love with Kate, and determined to make her his heiress, a proposal not at all distasteful to that pleasure-loving young lady Mrs. Pellypop was down at Marlow with her son-in-law, the Bishop and his meek little wife, and was already exercising over the entire household her despotic rule, until the whole house nearly arose in rebellion. The only one left in London who refused to leave it till Carmela took her departure was Vassalla, for that astute gentleman, seeing there was an estrangement between Carmela and the Australian, determined to turn it to his own advantage, and was always whispering insinuations against Monteith, until, one day, she turned round and asked him what he meant?

"You are always talking against Mr. Monteith," she said angrily, with a red spot on each cheek, "but I have never found him other than a very high-minded gentleman—besides," hurriedly, "what is he to me that I should care about him?"

"Nothing at all, my cousin," replied Vassalla smoothly, caressing his carefully-trimmed beard; "but I knew you liked him, and would be sorry if he conducted himself badly."

"His conduct has nothing to do with me," she retorted, sharply, "how do you mean he is conducting himself badly?

"Cherchez la femme," replied Vassalla, with sardonic smile.

Carmela's heart almost stood still. She turned very pale; but, with a great effort, managed to preserve her composure. So this was the reason of his coldness to her; he was in love with another woman, and had merely amused himself with her on the voyage. With her, Carmela Cotoner! The thought was madness—and she clenched her hands, while the hot blood flushed her cheeks rose-red.

"I don't believe it," she said, hoarsely.

"I can prove my words to be true," answered Vassalla, suavely;

"if you come with me to the Italian Exhibition you will see them there."

"How do you know?" she asked, raising her heavy eyes to his.

"That is a secret, my cousin; will you come?"

"No."

"Think it over; I will call again this afternoon," and Vassalla left the house humming a tune.

He knew Ronald would be at the Exhibition that afternoon, as he had met him in the morning casually, and Monteith had mentioned that he was going to take a lady to the Italian Exhibition, so the wily Maltese determined to turn the incident to his own benefit, and, if possible, rouse Carmela's jealousy—that once done, she would marry him, if only out of pique. He knew her too well to doubt that she would come, and he proved a true prophet, for when he called at the Langham at three o'clock, he found her waiting for him, dressed to go out. He, however, was too wise to make any comment, and, stepping into a hansom, they drove to the Strand, and went by the underground railway to the Exhibition.

Ronald was there, as he had promised to escort Mrs. Taunton, for the poor little lady was so grieved and horror-struck over her brother's death that she never let Ronald alone a moment, but was always urging him to go on with the case. It was in vain, he said, they would have to wait till the letter came from Malta before they could make a fresh move. Mrs. Taunton was fiercely impatient, and had accompanied the Australian not so much with the object of seeing the Exhibition as of discussing the case with him. They wandered about, in deep conversation, not heeding, in the least, the crowds of people around them. While thus engaged, Ronald did not see Miss Cotoner, who was standing by the Marchese, looking at him with a sad expression on her face.

"You see, I was right," whispered the Marchese.

"I see," said Carmela, in a tone of suppressed emotion; "but the lady may be only a friend."

"Oh, yes, a dear friend," he answered with a mocking laugh; "why, I tell you, he is never away from her."

"Who is she?" asked Carmela.

"I do not know," answered Vassalla, who knew perfectly well, but was not going to reveal his knowledge, "they are always together."

At this moment Ronald raised his eyes and saw Carmela. A sudden exclamation arose to his lips, and he made a movement as if about to step forward, when suddenly he drew back, and raising his hat with a bow, took his companion's arm and disappeared in the crowd. This action seemed to confirm Carmela's suspicions, and with a stifled sob she turned away, the Marchese following in silent triumph.

"Who was that lady?" asked Mrs. Taunton, when they were some distance away.

"A lady I know," he answered, evasively.

"And love?"

"Why do you think so?"

"That is, if you return love for love—I saw it in her face."

"Impossible!"

"Not at all, it's merely a woman's instinct; come, tell me, do you love her?"

"Yes," he answered, sadly, "too well."

"Nonsense," said Mrs. Taunton, rapidly, "no woman can be loved too well."

"No, I agree with you there—if she is worthy of it."

"And is this lady not worthy?"

"I don't know."

"How mysterious you are—it is cruel of me to keep you trying to solve the riddle of my brother's death, when you ought to be making love to that young lady."

"That is just it," said Ronald, with a groan; "if your brother had not been killed, I would not have doubted her."

"What do you mean?" asked Mrs. Taunton, breathlessly; "who is she?"

"Miss Cotoner."

"What! The sister of my brother's wife?"

"I don't know," he said, dreamily.

"You don't know—you don't know?" she said, with a quick, indrawn breath; "what parrot-cry is this—did she come from Malta?"

"Yes."

"Then she must be what I have said."

Ronald sighed.

"I cant tell till I hear from Malta."

"Does she know anything about my brother's death?"

"Good God! no," he answered, quickly; "how could she?"

"I don't know," she answered, between her clenched teeth; "but there is more in this than I understand."

"You don't think I am playing you false?" he said, sharply.

"No," she replied, in a kinder tone; "I don't think that—you have been so kind."

"I intend to find out who killed your brother, and punish him or her," he said, slowly; "and though I love Miss Cotoner more than my

82

life, till I discover this mystery, I will not speak one word of love to her."

"You promise me?"

"I promise," and he took her hand.

They were silent for a moment, and then passed out of the garden together, both absorbed in their own thoughts.

The woman's: "Will this love prevent him doing justice to my brother's memory?"

The man's; "Is Carmela aware that I know her relationship to Mrs. Verschoyle?"

CHAPTER XIV

A LETTER FROM MALTA

Julian Roper to Ronald Monteith.

Dear Sir,—I have now been here a week, and in accordance with your instructions, have lost no time in investigating the case entrusted to me; but the results, I regret to say, are far from satisfactory. On my arrival at Valletta, I took up my quarters at the Hotel D'Angleterre, in the Strada Sta. Lucia, made inquiries as to the whereabouts of Mrs. Verschoyle, and after some considerable difficulty, found that she was staying at a boarding-house in the Strada Cristoforo.

On learning this, I thought my best plan would be to take up my abode in the same house, as I could then learn with more precision the movements of Mrs. Verschoyle. To this end I went to the Strada Cristoforo, and found the boarding-house to be a very comfortable one, kept by a fat widow whose name is Signora Briffa. I secured very pleasant apartments, and took possession of them next day, much to my own satisfaction and that of the Signora.

At the table d'hôte I met the rest of the lodgers, who are a queer-looking lot, mostly Italians, with a sprinkling of English people. Among the latter is a Mrs. Dexter, the widow of a colonel in the Indian army, who has been staying in Valletta for the last fifteen years for her health, and being a garrulous old person, much given to gossip, knows everything and everyone. She is tall, rather thin, with sharp features—scanty, grey hair, and cold, grey eyes. In fact, she gave me the impression of being a decidedly unpleasant person, a presentiment which turned out to be true on my further acquaintance with her. She confesses to the age of thirty-five, though I shrewdly suspect forty-five, or even more, would be near the mark. She has one quality, however, which is of great service to me—she hates Mrs. Verschoyle with all the intense hatred of a narrow-minded woman. Her reasons are twofold. First, Mrs. Verschoyle is very handsome; Mrs. Dexter is not. Secondly, Mrs. Verschoyle is rich, whereas Mrs. Dexter is poor. Given these reasons, can you wonder at the malignity of her feelings towards Mrs. Verschoyle? As to the latter, she is very beautiful—I speak as an unenthusiastic man—tall, dark skinned, with clearly cut features, and magnificent, black eyes, she impressed me at once with an overwhelming sense of a strong personality. Looking at her in repose, she is a fine picture, but once hear her talk, and the charm is gone. Yes, her voice is very coarse, and sounds discordantly; in addition to which, she is insufferably proud—another cause of Mrs. Dexter's dislike—and has a very violent temper. She, of course, did not deign to speak to me—a mere English tourist—such, of course, is my character—but gave all her attention to Lord Francis Hurlington, a young nobleman who hovers round her like a moth round a candle. I hope he will not singe his lordly wings.

Seeing me, seated in the drawing-room all alone, Mrs. Dexter came and sat beside me, apparently out of good nature for one so forsaken, but in reality to learn all my history, and gratify her love of curiosity. I told her my history—that is, I invented a fictitious story, which proved that I ought to have been a novelist. In return for my confidence, she told me all about the inmates of the house, more especially of Mrs. Verschoyle, thinking, I've no doubt, that a skilfully coloured story might injure the lady in my estimation. I heard all about the divorce case, but as you are already acquainted with the facts, there is no need, on my part, for repetition, so I may as well tell you the story of Mrs. Verschoyle's life from the time she settled in Valletta after the divorce.

In the first place, she has an income from the late Mr. Verschoyle, and not caring to take a house, lived at first in lodgings; but such was the violence of her temper that she was turned out of one place after another till she found a haven of rest at Signora Briffa's, as that lady does not regard temper so long as the money is paid regularly. Mrs. Verschoyle has a sister called Carmela, who is at present in England, whither she went, on board the "Neptune." It appears she was in England before, but came out to Malta to live with her sister. They quarrelled, however, and Carmela, in a rage, left Mrs. Verschoyle and went to London, as you know, in the same boat as you did.

The Marchese Vassalla, who is her cousin, also went with her, though he has always been, and is still, good friends with Mrs. Verschoyle, and I shrewdly suspect, from hints conveyed by Mrs. Dexter, that the lady in question is in love with him. Having thus got a general outline of the life of Mrs. Verschoyle, I questioned Mrs. Dexter in detail, and here I was even more fortunate than before, as I found this excellent person kept a diary, which she agreed to show to me. You will wonder at my being honoured with such a confidence after so short an acquaintance, but the fact is Mrs. Dexter discovered—with a woman's instinct—that my mission was inimical to the interests of Mrs. Verschoyle, and she agreed to let me

85

see her diary, in order that I might secure anything that could be detrimental to her enemy's character.

I might as well mention that Mrs. Colonel Dexter, being quite alone in the world, and having very little money, agreed to accept a sum of money as a bribe, or, as she put it, a loan—loan or bribe, the fact remains the same—she took it. She likewise promised to observe profound secrecy, so, having thus secured her allegiance, I went to my own room and perused the pages of her diary, taking notes as I went along. The notes are as follows, but I am afraid they are of small value, as they seem—to my mind—to lead to nothing:—

EXTRACTS FROM THE DIARY OF MRS. DEXTER

April 29th.—Another quarrel! I knew it would lead to this. I wonder Carmela puts up with the insolence of her sister. No wonder Mr. Verschoyle divorced her; no one could live with such a bad-tempered woman. She says she divorced him, but, of course, I know the truth, though she doesn't think so. She puts me in mind of that horrid Major Penton's wife at Simla—the same bold way about her. I asked Carmela where Mr. Verschoyle was, and she said she did not know. Of course she did not, but I do; he's in Australia. Signora Briffa told me that Carmela was in love with Mr. Verschoyle herself, but he preferred her sister. No wonder they quarrel.

May 1st.—Mrs. Verschoyle is setting her cap at Lord Francis, and I can see very well is trying to marry him. He's a fool, I know, but not quite so foolish as to make her his wife, in fact, I think he rather inclines to her sister. I believe Mrs. Verschoyle sees this, and it makes her none the more friendly towards Carmela. I wonder how it will end?

May 10th.—Such a lot has happened lately. Lord Francis is gone, and Mrs. Verschoyle is furious. I am very glad, as she has missed her chance of a coronet. I believe he proposed to Carmela, and went away in a rage because she refused him. He has left for Constantinople in his yacht, and Mrs. Verschoyle would have given her ears to have gone also—the bold thing! The enmity between the sisters still continues, and I verily believe Mrs. Verschoyle would kill Carmela with pleasure if she could do so with safety. I overheard a curious conversation between them, and I wonder what it means. I was sitting in the drawing-room, half hidden by the curtains, when the sisters entered the room and began to quarrel as usual—a most delightful pair. I despise listeners, but I could not help myself, so had to overhear their conversation—unwillingly, of course; it will be best for me to put it in a dramatic form.

Mrs. Verschoyle: You know you loved him! (I wonder whom she means).

Carmela: Yes, I did, but it was only the fancy of a girl; when he married you I did not care a bit about him; (I see now, they are talking of Mrs. Verschoyle's husband;) but he was a good husband to you, and you might have made his life happy.

Mrs. Verschoyle: He betrayed me for another woman.

Carmela: Only after you made his life so unendurable that he had to leave you.

Mrs. Verschoyle: You take his part? I believe you are in love with him still.

Carmela: I am not, and you know it.

Here, Mrs. Verschoyle burst into a torrent of such abusive language, that, as a gentlewoman and a Christian, I had to interfere. Carmela left the room, and after Mrs. Verschoyle's anger had expended itself, she relapsed into sulky silence.

June 5th. Such a delightful man is staying here—Marchese Matteo Vassalla—he is a cousin of the sisters, and is waiting the arrival of the P. and O. "Neptune" to go on to England. I have made a discovery; he is in love with Carmela, and Mrs. Verschoyle is in love with him. How strange! Carmela always seems to stand in the way of her sister, and that does not mend the breach between them. They went out together and came back quarrelling—I suppose, about the Marchese—and Carmela said she was going to England in the "Neptune."

June 13th. The "Neptune" has arrived, and Carmela has secured her passage. She is going to Sir Mark Trevor in England, and will be escorted by her cousin, Vassalla. I should not wonder if they were engaged by the time they reach London. Carmela and her sister made up their quarrel, and went out together, then Carmela came back alone, almost crying and shut herself in her room. Mrs. Verschoyle's a minx; later on that lady came back in a fearful rage, I fancy she must have spoken to some one who differed from her; she tried to see Carmela, but that young lady very properly refused to be further insulted, so Mrs. Verschoyle shut herself up in her room. Carmela went away without saying good-bye to her, and Mrs. Verschoyle refused to come to dinner. After dinner, I went up to her room, and knocked at the door; it was still locked, and I could obtain no answer from her, so I went to bed early, having a headache.

June 14th.—Next morning Mrs. Verschoyle was not at breakfast, and sent down word she had a headache; no wonder, with the way she lets her violent temper run away with her. I saw her later in the day, and asked her why she did not answer when I knocked on the previous night. She said she was asleep and did not hear me. I did not speak to her again. She has lost both her lovers and her sister, and I'm not sorry.

Here all extracts from the diary likely to be of any use to us end, and if you will read them carefully, you will see that according to the report of Mrs. Dexter, faithfully given, Mrs. Verschoyle did not leave the house on the night of the sailing of the "Neptune," so she could not have been on board, and consequently must be innocent of the crime.

Now, of course, it is a debatable question whether or not Mrs. Verschoyle really did leave the house. You will perceive that she refused to come down to dinner, and stayed in her own room. After dinner, Mrs. Dexter went up to her door, found it locked, and could get no answer. Now, what was easier than for Mrs. Verschoyle to slip out of her room while all were at dinner, and the servants away in the kitchen, lock her door, to lead to the belief that she was still there, and go off to the ship, commit the crime, and come home again? Unluckily, Mrs. Dexter went to bed early, or Mrs. Verschoyle's return would not have escaped her lynx-eyes; so if she did go out as I surmise—and, mind you it is only a surmise—the servants might have seen her return. I therefore questioned the servants, but could get no satisfactory answers out of them, as they could remember nothing; not even money could sharpen their wits. In this extremity, I bethought myself of boldly asking Mrs. Verschoyle herself, and in the drawing-room, after dinner, I led the conversation round to the excellence of the P. and O. steamers, and asked her if she had seen the "Neptune"? She winced and changed colour a little, and then answered, "No." Mrs. Dexter then became my ally, and the conversation was as follows:—

Mrs. Dexter: Your sister went to England in the "Neptune?"

Mrs. Verschoyle: Yes, and so did my cousin, the Marchese Vassalla, but for all that, I did not see the boat.

Myself: Why—did you not go on board to say good-bye?

Mrs. Verschoyle: No; I had a headache, and did not leave my room.

Mrs. Dexter: Yes, I remember. I knocked at your door, and could get no answer.

Mrs. Verschoyle (quickly): I was asleep.

Myself: It was a pity you did not see the "Neptune"; she is such a magnificent vessel.

This closed the conversation, and left things as they were. You see, Mrs. Verschoyle denies that she left the house on that evening; so if this is the case, she can prove an alibi, and thus cannot be accused of committing the crime. I, however, am not satisfied with her denial; she winced when I mentioned the "Neptune"; moreover, I knew that her husband was on board, as she met him during the day; which, by the way, explains the passage in Mrs. Dexter's diary, that she returned in a rage.

To my mind, therefore, the only people who can definitely say if she were on board, are Miss Carmela Cotoner and the Marchese Vassalla; for even if she went on board secretly to see her husband, she could not have escaped notice by her sister and cousin. My advice, therefore, is for you to see either Miss Cotoner or the Marchese Vassalla, and find out if Mrs. Verschoyle were on board before the "Neptune" sailed; if so, we can pursue our inquiries; if not, we must turn in another direction.

As I have now got all the information I can obtain here, I am leaving to-morrow for England, and if possible, will get the stiletto used in the committal of the crime from the authorities at Gibraltar. I may add that I have obtained a specimen of Mrs. Verschoyle's writing to compare with the paper you gave me; and though there is a similarity, there is also a distinct difference; but then handwriting does alter in five or six years, and the best thing will be to submit the papers to an expert, who can easily tell if they were written by the same person.

I will call at Mr. Foster's rooms directly on my arrival in England, and report more fully.

Yours obediently,
Julian Roper.

CHAPTER XV

MARCHESE MATTEO VASSALLA

After reading Roper's letter, Ronald went to Foster's chambers and showed it to him. The barrister read it in silence, and then laying it down on the table, looked hard at Monteith.

"You see, I was right," he said, tapping the letter with his fingers; "Miss Cotoner is, as I thought, the sister of Mrs. Verschoyle."

"Yes," replied Ronald, quickly; "but she has nothing in common with her."

"Ah! you think not—let me see;" taking up the letter and glancing over it; "they both have tempers."

"Any woman would show temper, living with such a fiend as Mrs. Verschoyle," retorted Ronald, defending Carmela.

"They both loved the same man,—meaning Verschoyle."

"But Carmela's love for him was only a girlish fancy, as she says herself in Mrs. Dexter's diary."

"In short," said Foster, replacing the letter on the table; "you are so much in love with her that you cannot see her imperfections?"

"I am not blind to them, if that's what you mean," retorted Ronald, doggedly; "but all I know is, I love her, and intend to ask her to be my wife."

"Ah! well, as soon as this mystery is cleared up."

"I understand," said Foster, rising from his chair, and walking to and fro; "but, judging from this letter of Roper's, the elucidation seems as far off as ever."

"I don't see that—for, taking all things into consideration, I am inclined to think Mrs. Verschoyle is telling a lie."

"Oh! so you believe she was on board the 'Neptune' that night?" Ronald nodded.

"There's no proof."

"Certainly, not any actual proof," said Ronald, quietly; "but I think it is very probable that Roper's theory is correct, and she did leave her bedroom, lock the door, and then return without anyone seeing her."

"Well, the whole affair is easily settled—go and see Miss Cotoner, or Vassalla, and ask them if Mrs. Verschoyle came on board—they will certainly know."

"I don't believe Miss Cotoner knows anything about it," said Ronald, angrily; "if they quarrelled before leaving the house, you may be certain that Mrs. Verschoyle never came near her on the boat."

"But Miss Cotoner might have seen her sister."

"She might; but I won't ask her."

"Well, my dear boy," said Foster, rather annoyed at this sentimental obstinacy; "go and see Vassalla."

"Yes, I'll do that—he'll be able to tell me whether she was on board or not."

"No doubt—if it suit him to acknowledge it," retorted Foster, dryly.

"What do you mean?" asked the Australian, impatiently; "you think——"

"I mean nothing—I think nothing," replied the other, quickly; "go and see the Marchese Vassalla, and then tell me what you discover."

"And then——"

"Well, then, it depends on his answers regarding our next move."

Ronald put on his hat and gloves, then, taking his leave, went outside into the roar and bustle of Fleet Street. Through an archway he could see the quiet Temple Gardens, and could not help contrasting their solitariness and charm with the turmoil on the pavements.

"Hang it!" he said to himself, as he watched the busy crowds rushing past, "everyone here seems to live with their watches in their hands; I should not like to live here, but I suppose I'll have to stop till I find out all about Verschoyle's death;" and this last reflection putting him in mind of his engagement, he stepped into a hansom, and drove off to the Langham Hotel, to see Vassalla.

Vassalla was upstairs, in a private sitting-room, enjoying his breakfast, when Monteith's card was sent to him. Carmela had gone out with Sir Mark and his daughter, so the Marchese felt perfectly secure against the chance of Ronald meeting her. He dreaded the meeting, because disagreeable explanations might be made which would reconcile the lovers, and ruin all his carefully prepared schemes. As he looked at the card thoughtfully, he was rapidly running over in his mind the reasons which might make Ronald thus seek him. No feasible one, however, presenting itself to him, he told the waiter to show the gentleman up, and quietly went on with his breakfast.

"He has some reason for coming," he muttered, quietly; "and
91

I'll find it out; don't trouble yourself Mr. Monteith—friend or enemy, I'm equal to either."

He arose from his seat with an enigmatical smile on his face as the Australian entered, and held out his hand. The other took it with a slight reluctance which was noticed by the clever Maltese gentleman.

"Hum!" he thought; "not quite friendly, I see."

Ronald took a seat, declined the offer of breakfast and prepared to talk.

"Miss Cotoner is out," he said, coldly.

"Yes, with Sir Mark Trevor and his charming daughter," replied Vassalla. "Do you wish to see her?"

"No; I want to see you."

"Me?" the foreigner's eyebrows went up. "Well, I am at your disposal."

"It is about that murder that took place on board the 'Neptune,'" said Ronald, going straight to the point.

"Ah, indeed!" said said the Marchese, quietly; "a most interesting subject. Have you discovered anything yet?"

"Yes, many things."

"Such as will lead to the detection of the assassin, I presume?"

"I don't know," answered Ronald, shortly.

"That's a pity; can I assist you in any way?"

"I think you can."

"Then you may command my services," replied the Marchese, politely.

"Thank you; I will take advantage of your offer," said Ronald, glancing at the impassive face before him.

Vassalla bowed, folded his arms, and leaning back in his chair, prepared to listen.

"In the first place," said Ronald, "you knew him?"

Vassalla shook his head.

"No; I had not the honour of M. Ventin's acquaintance."

"His name was not Ventin."

"Indeed!"

"No; it was Leopold Verschoyle."

"Leopold Verschoyle," repeated the Marchese, looking at him sharply; "that was the name of the man who married my cousin."

"Yes, and from whom he was afterwards divorced."

"Exactly," said Vassalla. "I see you know the whole story; so he is the man who was killed?"

"He was, and I want to find out who killed him."

The eyebrows went up again incredulously.

92

"I hope you will succeed," said Vassalla, politely, "but in what way can I help you?"

"Do you know anyone who desired his death?"

"No.

"Not even his—wife?"

Vassalla rose to his feet with a bound, and looked fiercely at Ronald.

"This is an insult, sir," he hissed out between his teeth. "Do you dare to accuse my cousin of the murder?"

"I accuse no one," retorted Ronald, coolly. "I merely asked you if his wife would have been sorry at his death."

Vassalla threw himself back in his chair, with a short, angry laugh.

"Upon my soul, sir," he said, coldly, "I hardly recognise your right to speak to me about such a thing; but as you seem so bent on knowing, I think she would have been—very sorry, indeed."

"Oh! Then she still loved him?"

Vassalla cast his fine eyes up to the ceiling.

"Passionately!"

"That is curious," said Ronald, sardonically, "as I have a document in my possession, written five or six years ago, in which she threatens to kill him."

"Indeed, and how did you obtain such a document?"

"I found it among some papers left by Verschoyle with his sister, Mrs. Taunton."

"Ah!" Vassalla thought a moment: so this was the reason Monteith was with Mrs. Taunton; it was business, not love, that brought them together; well, at all events, he would not let Carmela know. After a moment's deliberation, he faced his adversary with a clear brow.

"Very likely it was written in her first outburst of jealous anger at being so betrayed by her husband; but I assure you she loved her husband deeply, in spite of the way he wronged her, and often spoke of him with affection."

Judging from the story told to him by Verschoyle, and the extracts from Mrs. Dexter's diary, Ronald thought this doubtful, but restrained his desire to give an opinion on that point.

"Did Mrs. Verschoyle come on board, the night the 'Neptune' left Malta?"

Vassalla glanced keenly at him.

"Why should she?"

"To see you and Miss Cotoner off."

"Suppose she did come on board?"

"She might have seen her husband."

93

"Impossible! She did not know he was on board."

"Yes, she did. Verschoyle told me he met her in Valletta on that day."

Vassalla drummed quickly in an annoyed manner on the table with his fingers, then answered abruptly,

"She did not come on board."

"Oh!" Ronald was disappointed; were all his suspicions groundless, after all?

"No; she was confined to her room all the evening with a headache."

This statement, as Ronald knew, tallied with Mrs. Dexter's diary, and he felt that, after all, it might be the truth, and that Mrs. Verschoyle had not been on board; in which case—who was the assassin?

Vassalla saw the expression of disbelief flitting across Ronald's expressive face, and arose to his feet.

"In order to convince you," he said, quickly, "I will show you the letter I received from my cousin."

"There is no need," began Ronald, but Vassalla interrupted him.

"Pardon me, there is," he said coldly; "I wish you to be thoroughly convinced that Mrs. Verschoyle was not on board, and could not have either seen her husband or have had anything to do with his death."

"I did not say she had," interrupted Ronald, hastily.

"No, but you thought so," retorted the Marchese, as he left the room.

Ronald arose to his feet, and walked hastily too and fro. He was wrong, then; Mrs. Verschoyle was innocent of her husband's death. Who, then, was the assassin, for no one else appeared to have had any reason to wish him evil. Vassalla himself? no! it could not be he, because he had no motive. The theory of Mrs. Verschoyle's criminality having been thus effectually disposed of, there appeared to be absolutely no clue to the perpetrator of the crime.

Vassalla returned with the letter, and handed it to Ronald, showing him at the same time the passage he alluded to.

"I was so sorry," said the letter, "not to have been able to come down and see you and Carmela away by the boat, but I had a very bad headache, and was shut up all the evening in my room."

Ronald handed back the letter in silence, but first thoughtfully glanced at the writing. It certainly resembled that in the letter written five or six years ago, but he could not recollect it with sufficient clearness to satisfy himself.

"You are convinced?" said Vassalla, as he placed the letter in his pocket-book.

94

"Yes," answered Ronald, "I am convinced; good-bye, and thank you for your kindness in answering my questions."

"A pleasure," said the Marchese, and bowed his visitor out with smiles, which, however, faded as the door closed.

"Curse that meddling fool," he muttered to himself, "why can't he mind his own business? but I've baffled him this time, and I'll baffle him again if he interfere."

CHAPTER XVI

CARMELA IS QUESTIONED

Of course Ronald went straight to Foster's office, and there made his report regarding the statements of Vassalla. The barrister listened to Monteith in silence, and, when he was in full possession of the facts, sat absently scribbling on his blotting-paper, much to Ronald's disgust at what he deemed his inattention. "Hang it, Foster," said the Australian, irritably, "I wish you'd say something; you've not lost your tongue, have you?"

"No; nor my brains either," retorted Foster, lighting a cigarette, "you'd better have a smoke; it will soothe you."

"I don't want to be soothed."

"Oh, yes, you do," returned Gerald, imperturbably; "try one of these; they are real Russian cigarettes."

In order to propitiate his companion, Ronald took one and smoked away in sulky silence. Mr. Foster settled himself deliberately in his chair, and fixing his clear eyes on Monteith, began to talk.

"What do you think of the position of affairs now?" he asked, knocking the ash off his cigarette.

"It seems to me that the game's up," retorted Ronald, sullenly.

"On the contrary, the game is just beginning to be interesting," said Foster, calmly.

"What do you mean?" asked Ronald, sitting up straight in his chair. "I tell you, Vassalla not only told me plainly that Mrs. Verschoyle was not on board, but showed me a letter in her own handwriting which confirmed it."

"Oh, yes," said Foster, satirically, "I must acknowledge it's all very beautifully arranged."

Ronald looked at him in amazement.

"What is beautifully arranged?" he asked, shortly.

"The plot."

"Plot—what plot?"

Foster arose from his chair, and walked slowly to and fro with his hands behind his back.

"I tell you what, my boy," he said, rapidly, "this thing is becoming more mysterious with every fresh discovery. Verschoyle had no enemy, as far as we know, but his wife; we have documentary evidence saying she intended to murder him, and he

96

was murdered at the very place where she was staying. Roper says she did not leave the house. Vassalla says she was not on board. Her own letter says she was confined to her room with a headache. Fudge! I don't believe any one of them."

"Then you think she was on board?" asked Ronald, eagerly.

"I'm certain of it. I ask you, as a logical man, whether a jealous woman like Mrs. Verschoyle, knowing her husband was on board the 'Neptune,' could resist the temptation of seeing him? Nonsense! I tell you she was on board, and if Vassalla says she was not, he has a reason."

"What reason can he have?"

"He wants to shield her from the consequences of her crime. He is her cousin, and blood is thicker than water."

"This is all very well," said Ronald, quietly; "but all your views are quite theoretical, and we cannot obtain a single particle of evidence to prove that she came on board at all."

"How do you know we cannot?"

"Well, there's Roper's letter—her own letter and Vassalla's denial. Who else can prove she was on board?"

"Miss Cotoner."

"Oh!" Ronald arose and went to the window. "I don't think so," he said, turning round. "If Mrs. Verschoyle quarrelled with her sister, it's not likely she'd go near her."

"Perhaps not, but Miss Cotoner might have seen her. You'd better go and ask her."

Ronald hesitated a moment, then made up his mind,

"Very well; I'll call at the Langham this afternoon, and may possibly see her; but I think it's a wild goose chase."

"We'll see," said Foster, shortly, returning to his books, while Ronald went off to his hotel, took a light luncheon, then dressing himself carefully, ordered a hansom, and drove to the Langham.

Carmela was in, so Ronald sent up his card to her, and asked for the favour of an interview. This, however, Carmela hesitated before granting, as she was very angry with Ronald's supposed treachery towards herself. Had she not seen her rival with her own eyes, and been told of Monteith's infatuation for that detestable woman, as she called innocent Mrs. Taunton? And now he had the bad taste to ask for an interview—well, she would grant his request, and would show him that she was not a woman to be lightly won and thrown over.

What consummate actresses women are! When Ronald entered her drawing-room, he expected to find Carmela pale and anxious, through fretting over his long absence from her side, and it was rather a blow to his self-love when she came forward with a bright, smiling face and outstretched hands.

97

"How do you do, Mr. Monteith?" she said, in her low, sweet voice; "you are quite a stranger."

Ronald muttered something about business as he took her hand, and then sat down, thinking to himself that this heartless coquette could never have cared for him. Carmela on her part, rang for afternoon tea, and then began to talk lightly of the most commonplace topics, much to Ronald's secret irritation.

"Sir Mark and Miss Trevor are out," she said, gaily, leaning back in her chair; "and it is a mere chance you found me in."

"When do you go to Marlow?" asked the Australian, abruptly.

"Next week, I think. I must confess I am a little tired of London."

"And Vassalla?"

She looked annoyed.

"I do not know what my cousin is going to do. Ah! here is the tea. Let me give you a cup;" rising and going to the table.

"Thank you," said Ronald, mechanically; "I want to speak to you on serious business."

"Do you indeed?" carelessly. "Milk and sugar?"

"Both," he answered, annoyed at the flippancy of her tone; "this business is very serious."

"It must be, judging from your tone," she replied, giving him his tea, and returning to her own seat. "By the way, what did you think of the Italian Exhibition?"

"What!" he said, with a sudden start. "Oh, yes, of course—I met you there when I was with Mrs. Taunton."

Carmela winced; so her rival was a married woman!

"I do not know her," she said, idly balancing her spoon on the edge of her cup.

"No," he said, bending forward; "but you know a relative of hers."

"Indeed!" carelessly; "and his name?"

"Leopold Verschoyle."

Carmela let her spoon fall with a crash, and turned her pale, scared face to Ronald quickly.

"Leopold Verschoyle?" she said, rapidly, while her breath came quick and sharp. "What do you know of Leopold Verschoyle?"

"I know he was your sister's husband."

"Was!" she smiled scornfully. "You speak in the past tense because of his divorce."

"No; I speak in the past tense because of his death."

"Death!" She arose to her feet with a look of horror in her dark eyes. "Is Leopold Verschoyle dead?"

"Yes. I will tell you all about it if you will answer a question."

98

She sat down again, pale but composed.

"And the question?"

"Was your sister, Mrs. Verschoyle, on board the night the 'Neptune' left Malta?"

"Yes."

Ronald sprang to his feet in horror.

"Are you sure?"

"Of course I am," she answered, raising her eyebrows. "My sister and myself had a quarrel during the day, and I did not say good-bye to her at the house, so I suppose she was sorry, for she came on board and took leave of me there."

"But Vassalla says she was not on board."

Carmela looked surprised.

"Why, he was with her all the time! I was separated from them by the crowd, and I did not see my sister again, but Vassalla told me he had seen her safely down the gangway before the ship sailed."

Ronald sat wrapped in thought; so Foster was right, there was some plot on foot; he made another attempt.

"But I saw a letter from your sister to Vassalla, in which she says she was not on board, being confined to her room with a bad headache."

"Why should my sister write such a letter?" asked Carmela, angrily. "I don't understand all this mystery; there was no reason why she should conceal the fact that she said good-bye to me on board the 'Neptune.'"

"I hope not," he said, gloomily.

"What do you mean?"

"I mean that your sister's husband was on board."

"What!" She rose to her feet, looking like a tall white lily; "how is it I never saw him? I would know Leopold Verschoyle among a thousand."

Ronald, seeing the deep interest she took in this man, became brutal.

"The reason you did not see him," he said, coldly, "was because he was murdered, and his name was Lionel Ventin."

"My God!"

A white heap on the floor, and Ronald bending over it, trying to bring her back to consciousness. He sprinkled some water on her face, and with a low moan she sat up, and pushing her dark hair off her forehead, looked confusedly at him.

"I must have fainted," she said, as he assisted her to a seat, "but the shock was too much. God knows I have forgotten Leopold Verschoyle many long day since; but dead! oh, it is too horrible."

Ronald sat in silence, not daring to say anything.

99

"Who killed him?" she asked, suddenly looking up.

"I don't know."

She clasped her hands over her knees, and looked fixedly at him.

"You don't know for certain," she said, slowly; "but you have your suspicions, and I want to know everything; tell me all."

Whereupon Ronald told her what had happened, and how the links were being slowly added to the chain of evidence that seemed to connect her sister with the crime. When he was done she was pale, but composed.

"It is very strange," she said, in her clear voice, "and I do not know what to say. I do not like my sister; she is a woman of violent temper, but I am certain she would not commit a crime."

"Then why does she deny being on board the night the crime was committed?"

"I cannot say, because she certainly was. I must write and ask her. I will also speak to Vassalla; there is something mysterious about this affair; but my sister must clear herself; it is too horrible that she should be suspected of such a crime; and this," with a sudden thought, "is why you are always with Mrs. Taunton?"

"Yes; she is quite distracted over her brother's death."

"Vassalla said you loved her."

Ronald sprang to his feet with a cry of anger.

"Then he lies; the only woman I ever did love, and ever shall love is——"

She placed her hand on his lips.

"Hush! Do not mention her name till the mystery of Leopold Verschoyle's death is solved."

"And then?" he said eagerly, catching her hand.

She drew it away quickly with a stifled cry.

"I cannot say," she said wildly, wringing her hands; "God only knows the end. My sister must defend herself from this charge. I will write to her at once."

At this moment a knock came to the door, and Carmela had just time to turn and conceal her haggard face when a servant entered with a telegram, and Ronald took it while the man retired.

"This telegram is for you," he said, holding it out.

"For me?" she said, turning and taking it from him; "what can it be about?" and she tore open the envelope, read the telegram, and gave a cry of delight.

"What is it?" asked Ronald, anxiously.

"I need not write to Malta," she said, quickly; "my sister is on her way to England."

CHAPTER XVII

MAN AGAINST WOMAN

Gerald Foster was eagerly awaiting the arrival of Ronald, in his chambers, for he was anxious to know what Carmela would say about her sister's movements on the night in question. He was pacing up and down his room, biting his nails, and casting impatient looks at the clock.

"He's a long time away," he said, aloud; "I wonder what on earth she's telling him. The worst of it is Monteith is so transparent that she will see through his motive at once, and, in order to shield her sister, will deny everything. They don't like one another, but for the credit of her own name she won't say a word—ah!" as a footstep on the stair attracted his attention, "here is my ambassador—I am anxious to learn the new move in the game. Well," as Ronald entered the room, "am I right or wrong?"

Ronald threw himself into a seat with an air of lassitude, and looked gloomily at the floor.

"You are right."

Foster gave a cry of triumph.

"I knew it; things are coming to a crisis my dear fellow, and we'll soon run this woman to earth."

"I hope not."

"You hope not—why?"

"Because I am anxious to marry Carmela, and I do not want to have a murderess for a sister-in-law."

"Whether it's made private or public, you are bound to have that," replied Foster, dryly; "my advice is not to marry her."

"But I love her, madly," said Ronald, raising his heavy eyes to his friend's face, "it would kill me to lose her."

"Men have died and worms have eaten them, but love did not kill them," said the barrister, cynically; "you'll get over this fancy in time—but come, tell me all about it."

So Ronald related his interview with Carmela, to which Foster listened attentively.

"I wonder what Vassalla will say to that?" he said, when the Australian had finished; "you see, Mrs. Verschoyle was on board after all."

"That does not prove her guilty of the murder," retorted Ronald.

"Then why does she try to prove an alibi?quot; said Foster, quickly. "Why, everything we find out only makes the case stronger against her. I should like to have an interview with her."

"That will be easily managed: she is coming to England."

"You don't say so! When?"

"Miss Cotoner received a cablegram while I was there," said Ronald, "and her sister is on her way now."

"What the deuce does she mean by running her head into the lion's mouth?" observed Foster, in a puzzled tone. "She must know that such a crime cannot be passed over in silence."

Ronald looked up suddenly.

"What are you going to do next?" he asked, wearily.

"Wait, and see Roper. He is on his way also, and I should not be surprised if he came in the same boat with her. So he may, perhaps, give us clearer information than we have already received."

Ronald groaned.

"This is the irony of fate," he said, in a dull voice. "Had I known how this case was likely to affect the woman I love best in the world, I would not have undertaken it, and the thing might have remained a mystery for ever."

"Possibly," replied Foster, pointedly; "but you forget, others might have taken it up. Besides, when you started in the case you did not love Miss Cotoner, and, moreover, did not know how closely she was connected with the author of the crime."

Ronald rose to his feet and took his hat and stick.

"I am going to the hotel," he said, "to lie down. I feel quite worn out."

"When may I see you again?" asked Foster, accompanying him to the door.

"To-morrow, when Roper arrives," and Monteith left the room without saying good-bye.

"Poor boy!" said Gerald, as he went back to his work, "he is very much cut up—and no wonder! Where will it all end? I expect in smoke; because the evidence is too slight, even to convict that woman. Well, we shall see when Roper arrives."

Ronald walked along the crowded street as in a dream, and paid no attention to the buzz of voices around and the noise of the traffic. So preoccupied he was with his own sad thoughts that he did not see that a man was walking beside him, till the latter spoke, and then he looked up with a start, and saw Vassalla looking at him with an amused smile.

"Eh, my friend," said the Marchese, lightly, "in what day-dream are you lost?"

"Not a very pleasant one," returned Ronald, coldly. "I was

thinking of our conversation this morning." Vassalla shrugged his shoulders.

"You might have had more pleasant thoughts," he said, with a sneer.

"I might," returned Monteith, emphatically. "I might have thought every word you said this morning true."

The Marchese changed colour a little, and drew himself up haughtily.

"Is this an insult, sir?" he asked.

"As you please," retorted Ronald, indifferently. "You will understand my meaning plainly, when I tell you that I had the pleasure of an interview with Miss Cotoner this morning."

"Indeed!" said Vassalla, his face looking as black as thunder; "and she said—"

"More than you would have cared to hear," replied the Australian. "She simply contradicted every word you said, and told me that her sister came on board and said good-bye to her, and that you, the Marchese Vassalla, knew she was there, and saw her down the gangway as she left the ship."

"It's a lie," retorted Vassalla, livid with rage; "Mrs. Verschoyle was not on board."

"Go and ask Miss Cotoner; she will tell you differently," said Ronald, fiercely. "You are playing a dangerous game, Marchese, for I have sworn to find out who killed Leopold Verschoyle, and, by God, I'll keep my word."

"You shall answer for this," hissed Vassalla between his teeth.

"When and where you please," retorted the Australian. "If the days of duelling are past in England, they are not on the Continent, and if you care to defend your damnable lies, I'll meet you anywhere you please."

"You shall hear from me, Monsieur," said Vassalla, hoarsely, and he walked away without another word.

"The black villain," muttered Ronald, as he strode along; "I believe he knows more about this affair than he cares to tell. I've been talking grandiloquently, I suppose; but I'll stick to my word, and I think I can hold my own both with pistol and rapier."

Quite a style of conversation of the time of George III., was it not? but all young men become romantic at times, and Ronald, brave lad that he was, meant all he said, being as much in earnest as any periwigged beau of the eighteenth century, though he carried a cane instead of a sword.

The Marchese Matteo Vassalla jumped into a hansom, and ordered the cabman to drive to the Langham Hotel, as he was anxious to see Carmela, and find out all that had taken place

103

between her and Monteith. It was necessary for him to do this, as he was anxious to win her for his wife, and the least slip on his part might prove fatal to success.

He was mad with rage when he entered the cab, but by the time it arrived at the Langham was quite calm and self-possessed, for he knew he would need to have all his wits about him in the coming interview. He dismissed his cab, and went up to the drawing-room, where he found no one. Ringing the bell he asked after Carmela, and was informed that she had gone to lie down; but, determined to see her, he sent up a message that he wanted her immediately on important business, and then calmly sat down to think over his line of action.

The waiter soon returned with a message that Miss Cotoner would be down shortly, and almost immediately, after he retired, Carmela appeared, looking white and wan in her long, white dress, with her dark hair hastily fastened in a dishevelled knot at the back of her head. She came quickly into the room, and would have spoken, but Vassalla gave her no time.

"My cousin," he said, rapidly, in French; "I congratulate you on the success of your interview this morning."

"What do you mean?" asked Carmela, haughtily.

"Simply this," retorted the Marchese, quietly, "that I have seen Monteith, and he told me to my face that you gave me the lie in your conversation with him."

"I did," she retorted, defiantly; "my sister was on board, and you had no right to say otherwise."

"Bah! You cannot see an inch before your nose," retorted Vassalla, taking out his pocket-book: "read this, and then see what your truth-telling tongue has done."

He handed her Mrs. Verschoyle's letter, which she read eagerly, and, having finished, gave it back to the Marchese, with a cold smile.

"I see, she also denies being on board," she said, quietly; "so you are both telling deliberate falsehoods; will you kindly explain this riddle to me?"

"That will be easy enough, my cousin," answered the Marchese, with a sneer; "I presume Monteith told you all about the death of Leopold Verschoyle?"

"Well?" she asked, turning a shade paler: though Heaven knows, poor thing, she was pale enough before.

"Well!" he echoed, mockingly; "don't you know that your sister was his wife, and, if it were known she had been on board, ugly questions might be asked?"

"I understand what you mean," said Carmela, clasping her hands, "you think that she—had something to do with his death."

"I did not say so."

"No; but you hinted as much."

"Then accept the hint I give, and deny that your sister was on board."

"What! deny my own words?"

"Certainly," he replied, coolly, "better than," significantly, "the other thing."

"I don't believe it; I don't believe it," she cried, vehemently. "Bianca did not kill him."

"How do you know?" he asked, pointedly.

"Do you also accuse her?" she said, turning fiercely on him.

"I accuse nobody," he said, coldly, "I merely tell you to hold your tongue."

"I will justify myself to my sister, not to you," said Carmela, proudly; "she will be here next week."

"What!—Is she coming here?" "Yes."

"My faith! What cursed fools women are," he cried: "write, telegraph, anything, only say she must not come."

"Why not?"

"Because there is danger."

"Danger!"

"Yes; that meddling young fool of a Monteith is trying to find out about Verschoyle's death; if he is successful your sister is lost."

"Is she guilty?"

"For the second time, I say—I did not say so."

"Is she guilty?"

"Yes."

Carmela gave a cry and turned away; this answer parted her from Ronald for ever. In an instant Vassalla was at her side—she felt his hot breath on her cheek.

"But, I can save her, I can save her!" he said hurriedly,—"on one condition."

"And that?"

"Your hand," and he put his arm round her waist.

"Never!" She tore herself away with an indignant cry; "do you take me for hush money?"

"Either that, or your sister will reap the reward of her crime, and our name will be dishonoured for ever."

"Think of your name alone," she said, imploringly; "you will save her?"

"On the condition I mention. I don't care for the name, I only care for you. Why will you not marry me? You think of the

105

Australian; he can be nothing to you. Would you marry the man who is hunting down your own flesh and blood; and would he marry the sister of a woman whom he knows is a murderess? Think again. I will save your sister and our family honour—on that one condition—you must be my wife."

"If not?" she asked, defiantly.

"Events must take their course. I will not interfere. If you marry me you will have an honoured name, and the satisfaction of knowing that you have saved your sister. If you refuse, you will lose your honourable name, your sister, and not even gain your Australian lover in return."

"Mercy!" she cried, falling at his feet.

"No!" He stood above her, calm and pitiless, stroking his beard.

"I will give anything but that," she murmured.

"I can accept nothing else."

"You are a devil!"

"Possibly. Your answer?"

She sprang to her feet with a face pale as marble, and clung to the mantelpiece for support; but though Vassalla saw she was weak he gave her no assistance.

"Your answer?" he demanded, pitilessly; "yes or no?"

"Yes," she whispered, and for the second time that day fainted.

CHAPTER XVIII

THE SECRETS OF THE PENNY POST

"Carmela Cotoner to Ronald Monteith.

"My Dear Mr. Monteith,—I write to let you know that in the interview I had with you yesterday, you misunderstood some of my statements. My sister, Mrs. Verschoyle, did not come on board with me to say good-bye, when the 'Neptune' sailed, but did so before I left home. You will understand why I write this letter.quot;

"Yours truly,
Carmela Cotoner."

* * * * *

"Poor soul," said Ronald, handing the letter to Foster; "I can understand—she knows her sister is guilty, and would shield her."

"Yes, I can see that," said Foster, glancing rapidly over the letter; "but how does she know her sister is guilty?"

"I don't know," said Ronald, blankly.

"Hum," answered Gerald, looking keenly at him; "let us look into this. In the first place, did you think she thought her sister guilty when you saw her?"

"No," eagerly; "I'm sure she did not."

"Then she must have seen some one in the meantime who told her the truth," returned Foster; "now, whom did you see in the meantime?"

"No one, except Vassalla," returned the Australian, innocently.

"Exactly," said the barrister, "you saw Vassalla, and told him you knew that he and Mrs. Verschoyle had lied regarding her movements on the night in question?"

"Well?"

"Well!" echoed Foster, rather annoyed, "can't you see? Vassalla knew Mrs. Verschoyle was on board, and also that Ventin was her husband, and told Carmela Cotoner all about it; so, to save her sister, she has recanted, and written a lie—a white lie, poor soul! for which she will be forgiven in heaven."

"Then what do you think of the whole affair?" said Ronald, eagerly.

"I think that Vassalla knows more about this affair than we give him credit," replied Foster.

"Shall I answer her letter?" said Monteith, after a pause.

"If you like," returned the other, shrugging his shoulders.

"Then I will."

* * * * *

"Ronald Monteith to Carmela Cotoner.

"My Dear Miss Cotoner,—I have received your letter. Believe me, I admire and respect your silence.

"Yours truly,
"Ronald Monteith."

* * * * *

"And what about your marriage?" asked Foster. "I'll wait till I see how this thing is cleared up," said Ronald, "and then——"

"Well?"

"Whether her sister is guilty or not, I'll marry her."

"That's a mistake."

"What! A mistake to marry a noble woman like that?" said Ronald. "No, Foster, she has been tried in the furnace, and has, to my eyes, come out pure as gold."

"Amen to that sweet prayer," quoted Foster, in his usual, cynical voice.

* * * * *

"Carmela Cotoner to Mrs. Verschoyle.

"I cannot address you as sister till I know the truth of this terrible story. Your husband was on board the 'Neptune,' and you saw him there, though you denied doing so. The question I now ask you is, whether this awful thing is true? Did you have anything to do with your husband's death? I know that you are cruel and proud, but I do not believe you to be so base as Vassalla says. Before we can meet again, I want to be assured that your hands are free from your husband's blood.

"Your sister,
Carmela."

* * * * *

"How did she find out?" asks Mrs. Verschoyle of herself; "no one could have known that my husband was on board. Carmela certainly knew I went to see her off, but how did she discover that Lionel Ventin was my husband? There must be some traitor in the camp, and that traitor is Matteo Vassalla. I will go to him to-morrow and find out the truth. If it is as I suspect, he'll wish he had held his tongue!"

* * * * *

"Matteo Vassalla to Carmela Cotoner.

"So you are down at Marlow? I hope you are enjoying the country, and getting back the roses to your cheeks, for I want my bride to look her best when married to me. London is very dull, and the only excitement is the arrival of your sister, from whom I have a note, saying she will call on me to-morrow. I will report the result of our interview in some future letter, though I hope to deliver it by word of mouth, as I am coming down to Marlow shortly, and will call on you at Sir Mark Trevor's place. Mr. Monteith is still in town, and still on his wild-goose chase, from which I'm afraid he'll derive very little gratification. I am the only person who can prove, absolutely, that your sister saw her husband on board, and had anything to do with his death, and I will keep my own counsel on condition that I receive my reward—your hand. Adieu, my dear cousin, till we meet again.

"Yours for ever,
Matteo Vassalla."

* * * * *

"So I have to pay the penalty of my sister's crime," said Carmela to herself on reading this letter. "In order to save her, I have to sacrifice myself! Oh, it is cruel, cruel! and yet what can I do? If she is innocent, I am free to marry the man I love; but if she is guilty, God help me! I can do nothing but sacrifice myself to save her!"

* * * * *

"Ronald Monteith to Carmela Cotoner.

"Is it true? I ask you, is it true, this rumour which I hear, that you are engaged to your cousin, Vassalla? Oh, Carmela, why have

109

you trifled with me in this way? You must have seen how I loved you, how I worshipped the very ground you trod on; and now you coldly throw me on one side, and accept the hand of a man whom you do not and cannot care about. Think of how you are ruining two lives—yours and mine—before you take this fatal step; once done, it cannot be recalled. I await your answer, and hope you may be able to deny this cruel lie.

"Ronald."

* * * * *

"Poor Ronald," mused Carmela, "I am cruel but only to be kind. He can never—marry into a family like ours, and the greatest kindness I can do him is to refuse him. God knows, I love him well enough, but he could never trust me, once he knows the secret of Leopold Verschoyle's death, and that he does know it I am convinced. He may blame me now, but he will bless me in the future; so I had better write and tell him that it is true, though my heart may break while I pen the words."

* * * * *

"Carmela Cotoner to Ronald Monteith.

"It is true! I am the fool of fortune, and this match is not of my own making. Forget that you have ever seen me, and your life's happiness will be the constant prayer of

"Carmela."

"My life's happiness!" said Ronald, with a sob. "God! She breaks my heart, ruins my life, and talks about praying for my happiness— so like a woman! so like a woman!"

110

CHAPTER XIX

WOMAN AGAINST MAN

Matteo Vassalla was in his sitting-room, walking to and fro with his hands in his pockets. The Maltese gentleman was very well satisfied with himself, as all his plans seemed likely to turn out as he wished. Carmela had promised to marry him, and, as she had plenty of money, this was very satisfactory to the impecunious nobleman. She did not love him, it was true; but then he agreed with Rochefoucauld, that it is best to begin marriage with a little aversion. And then he had the pleasure of taking the prize from under the very nose of his rival; the race had been a long one, and the prize had been awarded, not to the swiftest, but to the most diplomatic. Fate had played into Matteo's hands, and secure in the certainty of his good fortune, he strolled gaily up and down the room, humming to himself.

The only thing that troubled him was the coming interview with Mrs. Verschoyle, for he knew that lady loved him, and if she found out that Carmela was engaged to him, would do anything to stop the marriage. She would fling money, character, even life itself, to attain her ends, such was her passionate temper, and Vassalla knew she was a dangerous adversary. The only chance of getting the better of her was to keep cool, as she invariably lost her head, and gave her adversary time to espy the weak points in her armour, so the Marchese felt tolerably certain of winning the game; but still he had a bad quarter of an hour before him, and did not relish the prospect.

"Malediction on these women," he said, stopping in front of the mirror, and admiring himself; "why can't they accept the inevitable, and own themselves beaten? But no, this jade of a Bianca will fight to the last. I rather admire such tenacity of purpose myself, that is when I'm not the opponent in the game."

He went to his travelling writing-desk, which was lying on a side table, and, having unlocked it, took out Carmela's last letter, which he read carefully, the result of his reading being anything but pleasant to him.

"Wants me to release her," he muttered, throwing down the letter and resuming his walk, "not I—give up the quarry after it has been run to earth? My dear Carmela, you must think me a fool; without your fortune you'd be a pretty prize, but, with it, my faith, it's killing two birds with one stone—come in" as a knock came to the door.

111

"Mrs. Verschoyle!" announced the waiter, showing in that lady, and closed the door after him, leaving the two adversaries face to face with the feeling of battle in the air.

Mrs. Verschoyle, as she called herself, though she had no claim to the name, being divorced, was very like Carmela, only, not quite so handsome, while her expression was rather repellent, and her lowering eyebrows and firmly closed mouth warned Matteo Vassalla that she had come with hostile intentions. Matteo was the first to speak, and offered his visitor a chair.

"You will be seated, my cousin?" he asked, politely.

"When I choose," she said, harshly.

Vassalla shrugged his shoulders and produced a silver cigarette case.

"As you please," he said, carelessly opening it; "you will smoke?"

"No!"

"Drink?—there is excellent wine here."

"No!—I tell you," she retorted, viciously, "we can dispense with all these formalities, Marchese."

"Eh!" with a sudden lifting of the eyebrows, "why so precise, my cousin?"

"Because you are a villain!" retorted Mrs. Verschoyle, bringing her fist down on the table.

"So!" said Matteo, with a laugh, "perhaps you will give me your reasons for calling me such a name?"

"The best of all possible reasons, you deserve it!"

"Indeed—the world is not of your opinion."

"Bah!—the world does not know you."

"Ah! so you are going to be Madame Asmodeus, and unroof my house for the benefit of my neighbours?" And Vassalla, having lighted a cigarette, sat down and prepared to listen. He had not long to wait, for Mrs. Verschoyle burst out into a perfect volley of imprecations in Italian, to which, Vassalla listened very quietly.

"You're not improving," he said coolly, when she stopped for want of breath; "but all this is talk. I want to know the reason of your visit."

Mrs. Verschoyle took off her gloves, sat down in a chair, and dragging it up to the table, placed her elbows thereon, and began to talk rapidly.

"You Maltese dog!" she hissed between her teeth; "I know all—yes, all—did I not meet Signor Clement at the Strada Cristoforo, and did he not tell me that you were as the shadow of my sister Carmelo, and that you wanted to become her husband? speak, you traitor—is it not true?"

"Before I answer that question," sad Vassalla, calmly, knocking the ash off his cigarette, "first tell me who is this Signor Clement, that knows so much of my affairs?"

"He came from England."

"When?"

"Shortly after your ship arrived in London."

"Did he stop at the Signora Briffa's?"

"Yes."

"And asked questions?"

"He asked me none, but, ah!" with a gesture of impotent rage, "that Dexter, she gave him all the lies of me, I am certain."

"Exactly! and he told you that I was making love to Carmela, and advised you to come to England."

"How did you know?" asked Mrs. Verschoyle, looking at him with fiery eyes.

"Because I have my suspicions that this Clement is a spy."

"A spy—for what—on whom?"

"For murder—on you."

Mrs. Verschoyle grew deathly pale, she clenched her hands, and her two black eyes glared like burning coals at her cousin.

"Bah!" she said, at length, making a snatch at one of her gloves; "this is a child's story."

"No, upon my honour, it's not. I don't know for certain, but I could swear this man is a spy. Why should he go out to Valletta, lodge at the same house as you, and tell you this about me? Because he wanted you to come to England—because he is employed by an Australian devil called Monteith to hunt you down, and accuse you of the murder of your husband, Leopold Verschoyle."

Vassalla arose to his feet while speaking, and went over to the woman, who cowered in her chair like a savage beast, subdued for the moment, by a master's eye.

"It's a lie—a lie!" she hissed, tearing her glove, viciously; "who can prove I was on board?"

"Carmela."

"Carmela?" she bounded to her feet, her face working with fury; "she would not dare!"

"She has done so, and told Monteith."

"My God! my God!" cried Mrs. Verschoyle, stamping up and down the room; "Oh that my fingers were round her throat? She has taken my lovers from me, and now she'd take my life. Bah!" with a sudden change, "they can't prove anything. You can save me."

"Yes, but will I?"

Mrs. Verschoyle stole round the table, and laid her arm caressingly round his neck.

113

"Yes, you will, my Matteo. Think of the love I have for you. You will disappoint this bloodhound, when he thinks his game sure, and you will marry me. We will go back to our beautiful Malta, and there be happy."

This woman wooed with all the caressing fierceness of the South, her harsh voice sank to a liquid murmur, and her wonderful eyes lost their savage gleam, and became melting and tender.

"You will marry me," she whispered, softly.

Vassalla sneered to himself, then rising suddenly, removed her arms from around his neck.

"Impossible," he said, coldly; "I am engaged to Carmela."

Mrs. Verschoyle sprang back, her eyes blazing with anger, and dashed the fragments of her glove in his face.

"Ingrate! Traitor! Scoundrel! You shall suffer for this."

"Not at your hands," with a soft laugh.

"Yes! at my hands. I have your letters, written when you truly loved me. When you said you would kill——"

"Silence, devil!" and Matteo, his face set and stern, caught her arm.

"I will not be silent!" screamed Mrs. Verschoyle, struggling to get free. "You shall not marry Carmela."

"I shall; it is the price of your safety."

"My safety?" and she suddenly grew calm.

"Yes, Carmela would have married the Australian. I hated him, and wanted her. He has been searching for the person who killed Leopold Verschoyle, and the evidence all points to you. He asked me if you were on board that night? I said 'No.' I showed your letter. He asked Carmela? She said 'Yes.'"

"The fool!"

"I made her write a letter denying it. She will keep silent for your sake. No one but I can prove it. I will keep silent on condition that I marry Carmela. She has accepted me, and you will not refuse your consent."

"I will."

"You will not."

"Dog, let me go!"

"Not till you consent."

"No!"

Vassalla released her, and went to the door of his room.

"I will be back in a few moments," he said, coldly. "If you consent, and promise not to trouble me, I will save you; if not, you must take the consequences," and he went into his bedroom, and shut the door.

Mrs. Verschoyle recovered herself by a strong effort, and going

114

to the sideboard, poured out half a glass of brandy, which she drank off. This seemed to do her good, for she put her bonnet straight, smoothed her hair, and producing another pair of gloves from her pocket, put them on. Then she went round the room looking at things until she came to the table, whereon lay Vassalla's portfolio. She saw Carmela's letter, and first glancing towards the door to make sure he was safe, snatched it up, and devoured every word of it. Then, throwing it down, she ransacked the portfolio with nimble fingers, evidently to see if there were more.

"It is here! it is here!" she muttered, glancing rapidly over the papers. "Ah!" and with a cry of delight she picked up a letter and slipped it into her pocket.

Just as she did this she heard Vassalla's foot, and knew he was returning. Pushing all the papers back, she ran noiselessly to the mirror, leaving the portfolio in the same disorder as she had found it, and was arranging her bonnet strings, when Vassalla, dressed to go out, entered the room putting on his gloves.

"Your answer?" he said, sharply.

Mrs. Verschoyle turned to him with a smiling face.

"I am beaten. Yes."

He looked at her suspiciously.

"You mean it?"

"On condition that you stop the bloodhound."

"Agreed; and now let us go out."

"Where is Carmela?" she asked, as he held the door open.

"At Marlow with Sir Mark Trevor. Do you want to see her?"

"No; that is, not at present," she answered, going down the stairs. "Where does the bloodhound live?"

"Why do you want to know?" he asked, sharply.

"You needn't tell me unless you like," said Mrs. Verschoyle, haughtily; "I only asked from idle curiosity."

"I believe he is stopping at the Tavistock Hotel in Covent Garden."

"Oh!" carelessly, as they stepped out to the street, "this is my cab. Can I take you anywhere?"

"No, thank you," said Matteo, helping her in. "Good-bye at present. I'll see you again soon."

"I hope so," replied Mrs. Verschoyle; and Matteo walked away as the cab drove off.

Mrs. Verschoyle lay back, and smiled.

"You think you have won," she murmured, glancing at the stolen letter; "but there are always two to a game, my dear Matteo! You forget that!"

CHAPTER XX

JULIAN ROPER REPORTS

Julian Roper, alias Signor Clement, had come to London in the same boat as Mrs. Verschoyle, and had made profitable use of his time by inflaming that lady's anger. On the morning after his arrival he went to Foster's chambers, in order to make his report, and there found his employer, Ronald Monteith, in anything but a joyful frame of mind. Poor Ronald was very much cast down by the news of Carmela's engagement to the Marchese, though Foster tried to console him to the best of his ability.

"She is acting under compulsion, my dear boy," said Gerald. "Vassalla has been telling her that Mrs. Verschoyle is the assassin of her husband, and has demanded her hand as the price of his silence."

"How does he know that Mrs. Verschoyle is guilty?" asked Ronald, fiercely. "We have proved nothing! She may be as innocent as you or I, for all we know!"

"My dear lad," said Foster, shrugging his shoulders, "we can only go by circumstantial evidence in this case, and you must acknowledge, things do look very black against Mrs. Verschoyle!"

"Oh, why did I ever start trying to find out the murderess of Leopold Verschoyle?" groaned Ronald, laying his head on the table.

"Rather, why did you fall in love with Carmela Cotoner?" said Foster, not unkindly.

"We'll talk no more of this," said Ronald, hastily rising to his feet, "till we see Roper, and hear what he has to say."

So Gerald, pitying the young man's sorrow in his kindly heart, went back to his musty law papers, and Signor Jilted-in-Love looked out of the window in sulky silence. Yet not sulky, poor lad, for his heart was aching with the thought of his future life being passed without Carmela, having, with the fine chivalrous feelings of youth, vowed he'd marry no other lady.

Soon Julian Roper arrived, and was welcomed with heartfelt joy by both gentlemen, who sprang with alacrity to their feet to greet him. He entered quiet and impassive as ever, but his sharp, blue eyes took in at a glance the haggard looks of the Australian.

"You've been fretting, Mr. Monteith," he said, looking keenly at him.

"Bah! don't mind me," said Ronald, peevishly; "I'm a little jaded with London gaiety. Tell us all you have learned."

"I have not much to tell," said Roper, smoothly. "You read my letter?"

"Yes, we read your letter," echoed Foster, quickly; "that Mrs. Dexter, said Mrs. Verschoyle had not been out of the house. Monteith saw Vassalla, who corroborated the fact, and showed me a letter from Mrs. Verschoyle, which proved Mrs. Dexter's statement to be true, but——"

"Go on," said Roger, calmly, "I like but's—there is always a chance of another step being made when 'but' comes into the question. What did you do after seeing Vassalla?" addressing himself to the Australian.

"I saw Miss Cotoner," burst out Monteith.

"Humph!"—there was a world of meaning in Roper's voice, "and she said——"

"That Mrs. Verschoyle had been on board."

"I thought so."

"And afterwards denied it."

"Indeed!" Roper's eyebrows went up. "At whose instigation?"

"Vassalla's," broke in Foster, hastily, before Ronald could speak.

"I thought so," said the detective, calmly.

"Why did you think so?" asked Monteith, impatiently.

"In the first place," remarked Roper, complacently, "I had the honour of coming home in the same boat with Mrs. Verschoyle; secondly, I made her acquaintance as Signer Clement, and she liked me very much. I had frequent conversations with her, and told her I was a friend of Vassalla's."

"But you don't know him," said Ronald.

"All's fair in love, war, and—detective work," observed Roper, quietly; "I told Mrs. Verschoyle,—who I knew, from Mrs. Dexter's diary, was in love with Vassalla,—that the Marchese wanted to marry Carmela Cotoner, her sister."

"That's true enough," said Foster; "he's engaged to her now," whereat Ronald winced.

"The result was I aroused her jealousy, and she swore that she would prevent the marriage."

"But how?" from Ronald, eagerly, fain to cling like a drowning man to a straw.

"That's what I could not find out," said Roper, thoughtfully; "she said she could stop the marriage, and Vassalla would have to obey her. Now, what logical inference do you draw from this?"

"That Vassalla committed the murder!" said Ronald, hastily.

117

"Not necessarily," replied Roper, dryly; "but this, that if Vassalla knew she was on board that night, he also knew she committed the murder, and would therefore have a power over her; but her determination to stop the marriage shows that she must have some power over him; so that either she is innocent, or he committed the murder himself, and she can force him by fear of exposure to do what she wants."

"And which of these theories do you think is right?" asked Foster.

"I am doubtful," said the detective, becoming a little agitated; "but I—I have a third theory."

"Yes?" said Ronald, in a quiet tone, looking strangely at the detective.

Roper arose to his feet, and took a walk up and down the room for a minute, then turned to the young men, who were puzzled by his curious manner.

"Of course, it's only a theory," said Roper, nervously; "but—but—I can only tell you what I think."

"Tell us, in heaven's name!" cried Foster, rising.

"Then I think Miss Carmela Cotoner committed the crime."

"What?" Ronald sprang to his feet, and made a spring at the detective, but Foster caught him and held him back.

"Be quiet Ronald, be quiet," he said, firmly.

"A lie, a cursed, black lie," panted Ronald, glaring at the detective, who stood quietly looking at him. "What proof, what pro— D—n you, sir, where is your proof?"

Roper took out of his pocket-book the yellow scrap of paper given by Mrs. Taunton, and the fragment of a letter written by Carmela to her sister.

"I obtained these through Mrs. Dexter," he said, quietly placing them on the table; "look!"

Ronald looked for a moment, then reeled back into Foster's arms.

"My God! my God!" he sobbed. "My God!"

The handwritings were identical in every particular.

Foster went to a cupboard and got Ronald a glass of brandy, which he forced him to swallow; then, leaving the young man in the chair, with his face buried in his hands, he sat down at his own table, and began to speak to Foster.

"How did you make this discovery?" he asked, quietly.

"I remembered in Mr. Monteith's story," said Roper, "that both sisters loved the husband, and I wondered if it were not possible that the younger might commit the crime quite as well as the elder, though, I confess to you, I had no grounds for my suspicion. As I told you in my letter, I obtained a specimen of Mrs. Verschoyle's handwriting, and found, by comparison with this paper"—laying his hand on the yellow sheet—"that, though there was a similarity, there was also a slight difference. This began to confirm my theory, and by the kind aid of Mrs. Dexter, I obtained this letter of Miss Cotoner's, by which you will see they correspond in every particular."

At this moment Ronald arose from his seat, and staggering to the table, produced from his pocket-book the note written to him by Carmela before the "Neptune" reached Gibraltar.

Laying this down by the other papers, with a shaking hand, at the first glance it could be seen the handwritings were identical.

"It's true," groaned Ronald; "my God, it's true!" and he fell heavily into his chair again.

"And what is your opinion?" asked Foster.

"My theory," corrected Roper, "is this: I think Miss Cotoner saw her old lover on the boat, and committed the murder, trusting to the presence of her sister on board to shield her from the consequences of her crime.. I also believe that Vassalla knows she is guilty, and has threatened to tell unless she marry him."

"Yes, but what about Mrs. Verschoyle?"

"Oh! I think she knows that Carmela's guilty, and threatens to expose her, if she will not refuse to marry Vassalla."

"It all seems clear enough," said Foster, thoughtfully.

"Yes, but it's a d——d lie, for all that," said Ronald, springing to his feet, and oh, how haggard and worn his young face looked! "Look here, you fellows. I love Miss Cotoner, and I don't believe she's guilty. I think that cursed Vassalla is at the bottom of it all. I'm going to Marlow, where Carmela is, and there I'll act a part. I'll see her, speak to her, and find out everything, but I must have your promise not to move in the matter, till I tell you."

"We cannot promise," said Roper.

"Whose servant are you?" asked Ronald, fiercely; "will you do what I tell you?"

"The law——" began Roper.

"Hang the law, and you too," burst out Ronald; "if Carmela is guilty, you can't arrest her on the evidence you have, but she's innocent—innocent! d'ye hear? I'll stake my head on it. Give me a month to clear her, and if I don't do it by then, the law can take it's course."

"Agreed," said Roper.

"For my part," said Foster; "I don't care if the case stops now."

"I only want a month," cried Ronald, "and I'll prove her innocence, if I have to tear the truth out of Vassalla's black heart.

Because of a little superficial evidence, you believe her guilty. I don't. I love her, and I'll clear her; so help me God!"

Theatrical, no doubt, but both the men felt that the lad spoke from his heart.

"I'll have another glass of brandy, Foster," said Ronald, quietly.

He got it, and drank it.

'Tis but a step from the sublime to the ridiculous.

CHAPTER XXI

AT MARLOW REGATTA

Sir Mark Trevor's family mansion, as everyone knows, is in Cornwall, but, being passionately fond of the River Thames, he had bought a place down at Hurley, where he passed the summer months, and there entertained his large circle of friends. The idle, pleasant life of the river suited the baronet to perfection, and being a man fond of books and antiquities, he found the neighbourhood quite to his taste, much preferring the unpretending house at Hurley to his grand hall in Cornwall, and the pleasant vales and hills of Bucks to the wild Tors and iron-bound coasts of the west country.

Bellfield, as it was called—the name being an invention of Sir Mark's happy combination of his daughter's name and the fields which surrounded the house—was not a very large place. It had originally been a farm-house, and stood near the high road, while beyond arose the sloping hills with a fringe of trees on top, and down towards the river stretched broad fields, all yellow with waving corn.

The original portion of the house was built of flint, and Sir Mark had added to it, until the whole place looked nothing but a mass of gables covered with trelliswork and overgrown with creeping plants. But a very comfortable house it was, the favourite apartment being a kind of smoking-room which opened on to a glass porch, and beyond, a wide lawn, a gorse hedge, yellow with blossom, and a view of tall beeches and glimpses of distant hills.

The walls of the smoking-room were covered from top to bottom with cartoons from "Vanity Fair," only leaving one space where guns, daggers, swords, and other warlike instruments were displayed. Plenty of low basket-chairs, soft fur rugs, side tables with a generous profusion of pipes, tobacco, and cigarettes, and on the large table, near Sir Mark's writing desk, a spirit-stand always stood ready, together with an unlimited supply of soda and seltzer for thirsty boating parties.

There was a piano in one corner, with piles of new music, principally, it must be confessed, of the comic opera and music-hall orders, and over the piano a fox's head and brush, trophies of Miss Bell's prowess in the hunting field. Off this snuggery was the saddle-room, which the young men, and indeed not a few of the ladies used to vote "awfully jolly," in the expressive slang of to-day.

There were plenty of bedrooms, low-pitched and quaint, wide

staircases with unexpected turnings and twistings, and an oak-panelled dining-room, wherein Sir Mark's guests used to wax noisy at meals, but the favourite room of the house was undoubtedly the smoking-room, and in it on this bright July morning all the guests staying at Bellfield were waiting, ready to start for the Marlow Regatta.

And a very jovial party they were. Pat Ryan, having returned from the Emerald Isle, was talking his usual nonsense to pretty Kate Lester, who was stopping at Bellfield with her uncle, a gentleman who passed most of his time asleep. He had declined to go to the regatta, and was already lying in one of the low basket chairs pretending to read the Times.

Bell was standing by Carmela, who looked pale and white as she listened to Mr. Chester's chatter, giving that brilliant youth the mistaken idea that he had made an impression. Sir Mark was moving about, from one to the other, with his grave smile, and two young ladies, arrayed in white serge dresses, with jaunty straw hats, were flirting desperately with a young Oxonian called Wellthirp, but familiarly known as Bubbles, from his effervescent flow of spirits.

"We'd better start, I'm thinking," observed Mr. Ryan to the company; "it's a mighty bad thing wasting all this beautiful morning."

"You won't come, uncle?" asked Kate, going over to her avuncular relative.

"Not to-day, my dear; I'm a little tired."

"Begad, he's the seven sleepers rolled into one," said Pat to Miss Lester as they stepped out into the sunshine. "Come, Miss Lester, I'll race ye for a pair of gloves."

"Against what?" asked Kate, as he helped her through the gate.

"A kiss," said Pat, whereupon Kate blushed, and vowed she wouldn't run, so Pat set off, like a deer, by himself along the narrow path which led through the cornfield to the village of Hurley.

"How sad you are looking, Carmela," said Sir Mark, as he walked soberly along beside Miss Cotoner.

"She wants Mr. Monteith," said Bell, mischievously.

"Nonsense," retorted Carmela, while a flush came over her pale face.

"Then she'll soon be gratified," laughed Sir Mark; "for Mr. Monteith will be at the regatta to-day."

Carmela clenched her teeth. He would be at the regatta, and how would he meet her after all that had passed? The last time she saw him she was free, but now he would see her as the affianced wife of another. Well, she would wait and see. Their meeting must come sooner or later, so why not now?

122

The party went through the quaint village of Hurley, past the Old Bell inn with its antique gables and wide windows—through the remains of the old monastery, which was one of the finest in England, and along by Lady Bell Place with its old walls and picturesque, red roof, under which the conspirators of 1688 met to mature their plot for driving James II. from his kingdom.

Over the bridge they went, and found the river crowded with boats, filled with men in flannels, and pretty girls in yachting costumes, all waiting for the lock to be opened. Sir Mark's boats were below Hurley Lock, so they all went down, only pausing a moment to look into the lock, filled with boats, and presenting a blaze of colour. A number of young fellows were leaning on the great arms of the lock gate, chattering idle nonsense to the pretty girls in the boats below.

"I wonder how many engagements these flirtations at the locks have been accountable for?" said Pat, sentimentally, to Kate, as he handed her into his boat.

"I'm sure I don't know," retorted Kate, and a pretty flush dyed her cheek; though, to be sure, it might only have been the sun shining through her red sunshade. "Why do you ask?"

"Because I'd like one more to be added to the number," said Ryan, audaciously; whereat Kate blushed again, and was spared the trouble of answering by Bubbles telling the Irishman to push off, and not talk so much. Pat consented with an ill grace; for, versed as he was in affairs of the heart, he saw that Kate knew his feelings, and responded to them.

Kate and Carmela sat in the stern of the boat; the former steering, while Carmela sat idly gazing at the gay throng on the river, her thoughts far away with Ronald Monteith.

They passed Temple Court, embowered among trees, and had to take their turn in entering the lock, which gave Pat and Bubbles lots of opportunity to converse and chaff their friends. Indeed, it was really wonderful how many people these young men knew, and even Carmela smiled as she heard Pat's witty tongue running riot.

At last they got into the lock, Bubbles skilfully piloting them; and, as the boat sank rapidly to the lower reach, several ladies in other boats shrieked, but were pacified when the water ceased to fall.

"Begad, they're as bad as banshees!" said Pat; whereon he was once more told to hold his tongue by Bubbles, who was captain, and soon they were out again on the broad river, with the roar of the weir in their ears.

"An' would ye like to tow down?" asked Pat, persuasively, of Kate. But that young lady declined, on the plea of heat, so Pat had to give up his idea of a flirtation on the towing-path, and work hard instead.

"There's Bisham!" said Bubbles, as they passed the grey old abbey. "Where Shelley wrote his 'Revolt of Islam' floating in a boat under the beeches."

"Begad, I hope he had a lady with him!" said Pat, gaily; "there's nothing stirs imagination like a pretty girl."

"Your imagination is quite vivid enough already," said Carmela.

"There's Marlow Church and Marlow Bridge," observed Bubbles, still in the character of guide book.

"Where the bargees ate puppy pie," put in Ryan; "but here we are at Shaw's—shall we go on shore or stop in the boat?"

Both ladies preferred to go on shore, so, after making the boat fast among all the other crafts, Pat and Bubbles put on their coats, and handed the ladies out. Sir Mark's boat was nowhere to be seen, whereupon Pat proposed to go over to the Anglers' Hotel, and see what was doing there.

"I believe you want to drink," said Kate, severely, as they walked over the bridge.

"And small shame to me," retorted the undaunted Pat; "haven't I rowed ye down under a blazing sun?"

"I suppose you must be rewarded," said Carmela, with a smile; so Pat and Bubbles, nothing loth, went into the quaint inn, which bears the sign of the Anglers, and had two tankards of foaming beer.

"Xerxes wanted a new pleasure," said Bubbles, when he had finished. "I'd have given him a thirsty day on the river with a pot of beer handy."

Pat laughed at this, and they went out to join the ladies, who were seated under one of the big trees, talking to two men.

"Hullo!" said Bubbles; "where did these Johnnies spring from?" But Pat did not hear him, as he was running towards the taller of the two, and was soon shaking him heartily by the hand.

"My dear Ronald," he said, eagerly; "how are ye? I'm glad to have a look at ye again, and Foster, too. Oh, we are a happy family."

But neither Carmela nor Ronald looked very happy.

Pat introduced Bubbles, who speedily made himself at home, and both Foster and Ronald declining Mr. Ryan's hospitable invitation to drink, they all went over the bridge again to see the races.

A bright day, gaily dressed crowd, the broad, blue river crowded with crafts, and the green country and picturesque red-roofed houses on either side—nothing could be more delightful. Pat, Bubbles, and Foster, all ardent boating-men, shouted vociferously as the boats went shooting up the stream, their oars flashing in the sunlight.

And the cheers that rang through the air when the winning crew won by a boat's length were as hearty for the losers as for the victors.

Ronald, however, looked grave and haggard as he stood by Carmela's side watching the races. He kept glancing at her face, and saw that she, too, was pale and thin, while everyone else was bright and gay, enjoying the animated scene, only those two unhappy lovers were brooding over their sorrows.

"She could not have committed such a crime," thought Ronald, his eyes fixed absently on the bright waters.

"He can never believe that I am marrying my cousin willingly," she thought, with a sigh; "he must know that it's to save my sister."

"I had your letter," said Ronald, in a low whisper, in her ear.

"And you understood my reasons?" she asked, though her lips grew white.

He bowed, thinking she alluded to her crime.

"Is it true?" he asked, huskily.

"Yes; God forgive me, it is," she replied, thinking he was referring to her sister's sin.

Ronald gave a shudder, and turned away as white as a sheet.

"From her own lips," he muttered; "it is impossible; I'll ask her again."

Ah me, how often cross purposes mar our lives!

After that the party went down to the boats to luncheon, and Sir Mark, delighted to see the young men, asked them to dinner.

"We dine at seven," he said, hospitably, "where are you stopping?"

"The Crown Hotel," replied Foster.

"Then you'll come and dine with me to-night?" said Sir Mark.

"Yes," answered Ronald, eagerly, for he thought he then could speak freely to Carmela, "we shall be delighted."

Foster saw what his friend wanted, so gladly accepted the invitation, the more so, as he felt a decided inclination to improve his acquaintance with Miss Trevor, whose bright eyes had made an impression on his heart.

Ronald had no more speech with Carmela that day, and kept aloof from her, a fact she attributed to his knowledge of her engagement with Vassalla. The rest of the afternoon passed rapidly, and though there was to be a procession of illuminated boats that night, the Bellfield party said they would go home, and departed up the river in the gathering shadows, Sir Mark's cheery voice being the last heard. "Seven o'clock, my boys!" he sang out, "not a minute later."

CHAPTER XXII

THE TESTIMONY OF THE DAGGER

Ronald and Foster went up to the Crown Hotel, which is at the top of the principal street in Marlow, from which point two streets branch off to right and left, one leading to Little Marlow, the other to the village of Medmenham. A quaint, battered, old obelisk of stone, surrounded by an iron railing, stands in what is called the Market Place, and serves as a sign-post. The hotel itself, with its archway in the middle, which divides it into two parts, was mostly occupied with boating men, in their picturesque flannels, and as the young fellows went upstairs to dress, they saw the bar crowded with thirsty souls.

Ronald was ready first, and putting a light coat over his evening dress, went down to order a dog-cart to take them to Hurley, and then amused himself by observing the different people with which the place was thronged. Getting tired of this, he strolled through the dining-room to the quaint garden at the back, with the red brick walls, all softened by time and covered with peach trees.

"It's like the song," said Ronald, looking at all the harmonious tints, softened under the fading twilight of the sky, and he commenced to hum Hope Temple's song, "The Old Garden," when he heard Foster calling him, and found that gentleman waiting for him in the dog-cart.

"Jump up, my boy," said Mr. Foster; "we've no time to lose, it's past six now."

"All right," replied Ronald, pulling out his pipe; "wait till I light up." And, having done so, he sprang up to the side of his companion, and they were soon spinning swiftly down the High Street of Marlow.

"I know the way," said Foster; "so I'll drive."

Ronald nodded, by way of response as they went over the bridge, and they saw the river, dim and fantastic-looking below, while the lights were twinkling in the windows of houses, and the air was full of floating shadows. In front arose the great mass of Quarry Woods, with here and there a tall tree, standing out sharply against the clear glow of the sky. An owl hooted in the distance, and then there came the deep sound of a dog's bark, as the two young men drove swiftly along.

126

"Did you speak to Miss Cotoner to-day?" asked Foster, after a pause.

"I did not—exactly," said Ronald, hesitatingly, taking the cigar out of his mouth; "but she asked me if I knew the reason she was marrying her cousin. I said yes, and asked was it true?"

"And her answer?"

"Was, 'God help me, it is true!'"

"Humph!" said Foster, thoughtfully, "she might not have been referring to your thought that she killed Verschoyle, but to her own, that she marries him to shield her sister."

"Then you think she is innocent?" cried Ronald, eagerly.

"I don't know," replied Foster, "but I would certainly give her the benefit of the doubt rather than condemn her unheard."

"Condemn her!" echoed Ronald, bitterly, "God knows I'd give my life to prove her innocent."

"It won't be required of you, dear boy," retorted Foster, coolly, "the whole affair seems to be a deuced muddle, and it's my opinion that Vassalla is at the bottom of it; however, we'll see what success you meet with to-night."

Ronald did not answer, but, gripping his cigar hard with his lips, puffed away fiercely. They drove through the village of Bisham, up the long hill and down through the Temple Park, each absorbed in his own thoughts until they found themselves in front of Bellfield where a groom was waiting at the gate to take charge of the horse.

The two young men alighted and entered the house, where they were welcomed by Sir Mark, who, after they had removed their cloaks, led the way to the smoking-room, where Chester, Bubbles, Pat, and a young Oxonian, by name, Hammond, were assembled.

The ladies were not yet in the drawing-room, so the hospitable baronet proposed a glass of sherry and bitters, which was accepted by all the young men, and then they began to talk about the day's regatta until the servant announced the arrival of the Bishop of Patagonia, his wife, and Mrs. Pellypop.

The most stately thing in the world is, undoubtedly, a swan, the next a Bishop; and when the worthy churchman walked in, tall and dignified, no one would have thought how he quailed before his mother-in-law. But such is the superior force of women that they can subdue even the haughtiest natures to their yoke—if they go the right way about it.

My Lord Bishop was very affable and very condescending, and when they went to join the ladies in the drawing-room, Pat pronounced him a good sort, and he, whose experience was extensive, knew a good sort when he saw one.

Mrs. Pellypop, tall and majestic, in black velvet and lace; Mrs.

Bishop, timid and nervous, hid herself under the matrimonial wing, and all the ladies looked even more charming in evening dress than during the day. At the sound of the gong, Sir Mark gave his arm to Mrs. Pellypop; he ought to have done so to the Bishop's lady, but then, Mrs. Pellypop always insisted on going first. The Bishop escorted Miss Trevor as the hostess, and Ronald found himself walking by Carmela.

They spoke very little to one another, Carmela talking principally to Bubbles, who sat beside her, and Ronald listening to the talk of a young lady next to him, who was a Girton girl, and thought she knew everything, whereas she knew nothing,—not even what a bore she was. Ronald thought the dinner was interminable; but it came to an end, as all things must, and the ladies followed Bell out of the room. The gentlemen, left to themselves, waxed merry over their wine; but were restrained from transgression by the presence of the Bishop, which that astute prelate quickly perceived, and left the room, followed by Sir Mark. Truth to tell, both gentlemen were anxious to escape in order to discuss a high church question then vexing the land.

"Mr. Ryan," said Sir Mark, as he left the room, "you can look after my guests."

"Faith, I will," cried Pat, taking the host's chair, "now then, boys, fill up, and no heel taps. Ronald, my boy, you're like a death's head; pass the claret, and don't be bringing your Egyptian mummies to the feast."

Under the influence of Pat, everyone woke up, and the wine was circulated, and also several stories, the morality of which was doubtful. After they had had enough wine, all the gentlemen adjourned to the drawing-room, where they found the Girton girl at the piano, wailing out the last new sentimental ballad, called "Columbine," which was very milk-and-watery, but useful in keeping the conversation going.

Then Mrs. Bishop tickled the piano in a mild, clerical way, playing "The Maiden's Prayer," as taught to her by Mrs. Pellypop, who learned it in her youth, somewhere about the reign of George III. Carmela was asked to sing, but refused, whereupon Pat sat down and sang, "I love a lubly gal," the melody of which brought all sorts of memories to Ronald's heart, as he remembered the days on board the "Neptune." He looked at Carmela, but saw she had arisen from her seat, and had gone out into the moonlight. Ronald sprang to his feet, and, snatching up a light cloak, ran out to place it on her shoulders.

"You will catch cold, Miss Cotoner," he said politely placing it round her.

Carmela accepted his attention passively, and they walked in silence round the house, until they came to the lawn. A ruddy glare of light blazed across it, which proceeded through the open door of the smoking-room, and it looked so warm and comfortable that they both moved simultaneously towards it, and stepped in.

"It will be warmer here," said Ronald, ceremoniously removing the cloak from his companion's shoulders, while she knelt in front of the fire, and spread out her hands to the blaze. The Australian leaned against the mantelpiece, tall and stately, and looked sadly at the girl at his feet.

"Yes," replied Carmela, slowly; "it will be—why do you speak to me so coldly?" she asked, suddenly.

"How would you have me speak?" he said, bitterly; "you cannot expect me to say much to another man's promised wife."

This was brutal—she arose to her feet.

"I did not expect that from you," she said. "You are unjust; I am forced into this."

"You are not," he began but she stopped him.

"I think we will go to the drawing-room, Mr. Monteith," she interrupted; "will you give me your arm? this is a pleasant room," with an effort at gaiety.

"Yes, very," he replied. They were both acting a part.

"Look at all these guns and daggers," said Carmela, stopping before them, "and there's a stiletto; get it down, will you, Mr. Monteith?"

Ronald took down the weapon, overcome with vague emotions. A stiletto, the very weapon she had used to— But, no—it could not be true.

"It's very pretty," said Carmela, taking it to the lamp to examine it. "I had one once with an ivory handle—the head of Bacchus surrounded with bunches of grapes."

Ronald gave a cry. She was describing the very stiletto by which Verschoyle had been killed. Great heavens! could it be that she was guilty after all?

"Head of Bacchus—grapes! was—was that yours?" he stammered.

"Yes," she replied, laying down the weapon on the table, and looking at him in a puzzled manner.

"When did you see it last?

"Oh, not for many years; it has been lost for a long time."

Was she trying to shelter herself under the cloak of a lie? Ronald was determined to know the worst. He sprang forward and caught her wrist, she recoiled with a cry of alarm.

129

"Now, tell me the truth." panted Ronald, his eyes blazing fiercely; "tell me the truth, I will not betray you."

"What do you mean?"

"Did you kill him?"

"Kill him—whom?"

"Leopold Verschoyle."

"Are you mad?"

She flung away his hand, and drawing herself up to her full height, looked like an angry goddess at the man who thus insulted her. But Ronald was too excited to heed her, and his words came pouring out in one torrent.

"Yes, I am mad—mad, to believe anything against you, who are as pure as an angel. I'm only a poor devil who loves you, and want you to tell me all you know about this murder, so that I can save you."

"Save me—murder!"

She reeled a little, and caught hold of the table for support.

"Look! look!" cried Ronald, pulling out his pocket-book with the fatal paper, which he had brought on purpose; "look here"—spreading it out—"your writing—your writing."

Carmela glanced at it, and a film came over her eyes.

"Yes, it's my writing—seven—seven years ago."

"Then the stiletto by which he was killed, you have described it. You were on board; you recognised him."

"I did not." She spoke the words firmly. "No, until you told me the other day who the murdered man was, I had no more idea than you had at Malta that Lionel Ventin was Leopold Verschoyle. I did write that note when I was mad with the treatment I had received. I was only a girl, and acted foolishly, as girls will. I did have such a stiletto, but I have not seen it for years. I gave it to my cousin Vassalla about five years ago."

"Vassalla!" Ronald looked up suddenly. "Are you sure?"

"Yes, he took a fancy to it, and I presented it to him. Did you believe me guilty?" suddenly.

"No, on my soul I did not."

"Can I believe you?"

"Yes,—appearances were against you, but I swore you were—innocent. I told the detective so."

"Detective! Is a detective employed?"

"Yes."

"By you?—don't deny it. I see it in your face. Oh, God!" wringing her hands; "What am I to do? You will ruin my sister!"

Ronald suddenly grew calm.

"Carmela, you know I love you?"

130

"Don't speak of love at such a time."

"I must; I believe I can save your sister."

"You can?"

"Yes, I think so."

She clasped her hands with a gesture of entreaty.

"Oh, if you only could," she cried passionately, "I would not then be forced to marry Vassalla!"

"That is one of my reasons for trying to save her," he said. "I do not want you to sacrifice yourself in this way—but we must not talk, we must act"; and he struck the bell on the table.

"What would you do?" she asked.

"You must tell my friend Foster all you know about your sister's marriage; he is a lawyer, and will find a way out of this dilemma."

The servant appeared.

"Tell Mr. Foster to come here."

The servant disappeared.

"How can you save my sister," she asked, quickly; "is she innocent?"

"I don't know," he replied evasively; "but even if she is guilty, I'll save her."

Mr. Foster entered the room.

"Well," said that gentleman, "what's the matter?"

"Miss Cotoner would like to tell you a story," said Ronald quietly.

Carmela sat down, and so did Foster, who was now all attention, while Ronald leaned against the mantelpiece, and listened eagerly.

"This," thought Foster, as he settled himself, "is the beginning of the end."

CHAPTER XXIII

A LOOK INTO THE PAST

Someone in the drawing-room was playing a valse, "Love's Sorrow," and in after years Ronald could never hear the melody without recalling the scene in the smoking-room at Bellfield. The eminently masculine characteristics of the room, the steady glow of the lamp, the quiet, cold moonlight outside, and those two figures seated before him. His friend Foster, with his keen eyes fixed on Carmela,—the woman he loved, seated in the low chair looking like a statue, with her white dress and rigid face, and the mockery of that brilliant valse music sounding fitfully at intervals, while this bitter scene was taking place.

"I will tell you all I know about Leopold Verschoyle," said Carmela, in low, steady tones, clasping her hands before her; "though I do not know I can throw any light upon the subject of his murder, but you can hear and judge for yourselves.

"When I first met Leopold he was a fascinating man of the world, and I but a simple girl of nineteen. My sister was four years older, and we both fell in love with him. He paid his addresses to both of us, and I think it was then my sister first began to hate me, though heaven knows she had no cause to do so, for he married her, and left me to make the best of my—as I thought then—broken heart. I have recovered, however, and now that the scales have fallen from my eyes, I see that Leopold Verschoyle was not worthy of being loved, and as long as he gratified his own selfish passions, cared nothing for the lives he wrecked.

"When he married my sister, in the first burst of passion, I wrote that paper"—pointing to the table—"but it was merely an outcome of girlish anger. I wrote it blindly, and did not mean what I said; indeed, I had forgotten all about it till Mr. Monteith showed it to me just now. Why Leopold Verschoyle kept it I don't know, unless to laugh at my folly and petulance. Well, I went to England after he deceived me, and stayed with Sir Mark Trevor; but I must tell you that my sister had another lover, Matteo Vassalla."

"But I thought he loved you!" broke in Ronald, impetuously.

"Now," she replied quietly, "but seven years ago it was my sister, and he went nearly out of his mind when he found her married. He used to rave to me that he would kill Verschoyle, but, of course, this was merely a fit of madness, the same as came over me

132

when I wrote that letter. He also left Malta, and travelled in the East, and before he went I gave him the stiletto for a keepsake. We did not see one another for many years, as I lived quietly in England.

"As for the rest, you know all about my sister's unhappy life; how her husband separated from her and went with Elsie Macgregor; then she found out his infidelity and obtained the divorce. He went to Australia with Elsie Macgregor, whom, I heard, he had made his wife, and now——"

"She is dead!" said Foster, slowly.

"Unlucky woman!" replied Carmela, calmly; "but then everyone who had to do with Leopold Verschoyle was unlucky. When my sister obtained her divorce, she asked me to come and live with her in Valletta, and as I was alone in the world I agreed to do so. But we did not get on well together; she hated me, and always said that Leopold Verschoyle loved me best."

"Did she threaten him in any way?" asked Foster, eagerly.

"Not in any special way; she raved and stormed, but then she was always doing that; her molehills were mountains. I bore with her as long as I could, till Vassalla came home and wanted to marry me. My sister, however, fell in love with him, and longed for that which she had formerly rejected. I did not like my cousin, and told him so, but he would not be discouraged, and of course this only made matters worse.

"When the 'Neptune' arrived, I had already taken my passage, and was much surprised when Vassalla told me he was leaving Malta also; it was too late to go in another boat, or I would certainly have done so. My sister had a quarrel with me on that day when you," to Monteith, "saw us on the Barraca, and I left her, and walked home to our lodgings. I never saw her again till we met on board before the boat left."

"Then she was on board?" asked Ronald, quickly.

"Yes, it is no use me denying it, she was on board, and appeared to be very excited; she said she had seen Leopold in Valletta that day, but did not tell me he was on board the boat; then she, together with Vassalla, became separated from me in the crowd, and I never saw her again. After the boat sailed, I asked Vassalla why she had not said good-bye, and he informed me that the crowd was so great she could not find me, and went on shore as the last bell rang."

"Was Vassalla excited when he spoke to you?" asked the barrister, thoughtfully.

"No; as cool and quiet as he generally is."

"When the murder was discovered, did he say anything—make any remark?"

"No; except to mention that a passenger, called Mr. Ventin, had been killed."

"Did he see the body?" said Foster, turning to Ronald.

"I don't think so," replied Ronald doubtfully; "very few saw the body; but, of course, he must have known that Verschoyle was on board."

"How so?"

"Because Verschoyle was leaning over the side of the ship when the new passengers were coming up, and he must have recognised him, especially when Mrs. Verschoyle told him she had seen her former husband; he would then be on the look-out for him."

"Humph!—yes—no doubt," replied Foster, thoughtfully. "Can you tell us anything else, Miss Cotoner?"

"Nothing," she answered, rising to her feet, "except that Vassalla told me my sister had committed the crime, and instructed me to deny seeing her on board, which I did—I wrote to you," turning to to Monteith.

"Yes, I understood your letter," he said, gently; and Carmela flashed a grateful look at him.

"Vassalla said he was the only one who could bring the crime home to my sister," she went on, "and made me promise to marry him as the price of his silence."

"But you will not do so?" cried Monteith.

"What can I do?" she said, helplessly. "I cannot see my sister accused of such a crime, when I know it is in my power to prevent it."

"He won't accuse her," broke in Foster, bluntly.

"Then you think she is innocent?" said Carmela, joyfully.

"I don't know that," answered Foster; "the whole affair seems to lie between your sister and Vassalla. He knows more about this affair than we think. Your sister is in England—is she not?"

"Yes."

"You have not seen her?"

"No; I refused, until she cleared herself of this charge."

"Do you know why she came here?"

"No."

"Because the detective we sent out told her that the Marchese wanted to marry you, and she came to stop the marriage."

"Bah!" said Carmela, scornfully, "she knows I don't care for Vassalla."

"True enough," answered Foster, quietly; "but she knows Vassalla cares for you. What will be the consequence? She will try and make Vassalla break off the marriage. If he refuse——"

"Well?" they both cried, in a breath.

134

"My dear young people," said Foster, in rather an annoyed tone, "don't you see what must happen? Mrs. Verschoyle will lose her head, and they will quarrel, and when thieves fall out, honest men get their due."

"But I don't see——" began Ronald.

"Of course, you don't," said Gerald, with a dry laugh; "but if that interview has taken place, I'll bet you what you like one of us three will hear from Mrs. Verschoyle, for if her temper is what you say, she'll move heaven and earth to stop the marriage."

"I hope so," said Carmela, sadly.

"Of course, she will," replied Foster, cheerfully; "she will throw away honour, fortune, life itself, to obtain her ends, if she's so madly in love. When a man starts for the Devil, he generally arrives, but when a woman begins she runs past the Devil—and goes God knows where. Now, let us return to the drawing-room."

So, after this serious interview, they all went back to the drawing-room, where they were questioned by everyone about their past.

"We've been in the smoking-room," said Carmela, with a smile, her heart now feeling lighter than it had been for many a day.

"Oh!" said Pat, in mock horror; "do Maltese ladies smoke?"

"You ought to know, Pat," retorted Ronald; "you saw enough of the sex in Valletta."

"It's my kindly heart," retorted Pat, who was never at a loss for an answer. "Sure, I didn't like to see the poor things castin' such longing glances, without responding to 'em."

Everyone but Mrs. Pellypop laughed at this, and she snorted reprovingly.

"With such views, Mr. Ryan," said that good lady, "I hope you will never marry."

"Why not?" asked Ryan, glancing at Kate; "my natural inclination for matrimony is strong."

"I hope your wife will be," said Ronald, with a laugh; "or she'll never be able to keep you in order."

Foster had established himself by Bell, who did not appear to discourage the advances of the young barrister, though her attention was somewhat distracted by Bubbles, who sat next to her. Seeing this, Pat, who had a fellow-feeling for lovers, drew the young man away.

"Bubbles," he said, "was it you that sat for that Pear's soap picture?"

"Of course," retorted Bubbles; "I was the original infant."

And indeed he did not look unlike the picture, with his beardless face and curly hair.

135

"Faith," said Mr. Ryan, "it's a mighty original infant you are, anyhow."

"Well, we can't all be Irish," said Bubbles, satirically.

"And a great pity it is ye can't," retorted Pat, calmly; "the finest nation under the sun. Did ye ever hear anything that touched your heart like Irish music?"

"Sing us some, and then we'll judge," said Sir Mark, suddenly interposing.

So Pat, nothing loth, went to the piano, and sang Moore's exquisite song, "She is far from the Land," in such a pathetic manner that he cast quite a gloom over the company, but restored the joyous tone by dashing into "Garryowen."

At the conclusion of Pat's ditties, Ronald and Foster arose to go, in spite of a chorus that it was early. But Mrs. Pellypop, on behalf of the clerical party, said it was late.

"Begad, the night's young, and the liquor's plentiful," said Pat, impudently.

"I never touch spirits," said Mrs. Pellypop, majestically.

"More's the pity," retorted Pat; "it 'ud keep the night air out, anyhow."

Mrs. Pellypop deigned no response to this flippancy, but sailed out of the room, and shortly afterwards departed with the Bishop, and her daughter.

Ronald and Foster had a glass of whisky and soda each while their dog-cart was being brought round, and then went off, Ronald promising to call next day.

"And you won't forget what I told you," said Carmela, as he went.

"No," replied Ronald, pressing her hand; "and mind you let me know when Vassalla comes down."

They drove off in the moonlight, in silence for a time, and then Foster said—

"What a charming girl is Miss Trevor."

"Oh, ho!" from Monteith: "so you've lost your heart?"

"And why not?" retorted Foster; "you are not the only person privileged to lose your heart."

"Well, I hope your course of true love will run smoother than mine," sighed Ronald.

"My dear old boy," said Foster, "yours will be all right. I've got a presentiment that we shall hear from Mrs. Verschoyle."

"Do you think she is guilty?" asked Ronald.

"I don't know, but whether or no, she'll not let this marriage take place."

"But she can't stop it."

"Can't she? she knows more, perhaps, than we think. How is it Vassalla's dagger was found in the dead man's breast?"

"But you don't think"—began Ronald, when Foster interrupted him.

"I think nothing," he retorted, whipping up the horse, "except that we'll hear from Mrs. Verschoyle."

Events proved him a true prophet, for on arrival at the Crown Hotel there was a letter waiting for Ronald, which he opened and read, then passed it to Foster.

"Didn't I tell you?" said the lawyer, when he read it.

"Yes—I believe the end is nearer than we think."

The letter said that Mrs. Verschoyle would call on Mr. Monteith at the Crown Hotel, Great Marlow, the next day at three o'clock.

So, Foster's presentiment was true after all.

CHAPTER XXIV

MRS. VERSCHOYLE PAYS A VISIT

Next morning, when Ronald awoke, he was very much exercised in his mind as to the reason of Mrs. Verschoyle's visit, and wondered what she wanted to see him about.

"I wonder if she wants me to marry Carmela?" he thought; "of course, if she's in love with Vassalla, she'll be only too anxious to get Carmela disposed of. She did not commit the murder, or she wouldn't be such a fool as to come to England."

When he finished dressing, Mr. Monteith went downstairs into the dining-room, a pleasant apartment that opened, by French windows, on to the quaint old garden with the red-brick walls. He lighted a cigarette and walked slowly up and down waiting for Foster to come to breakfast, and was speedily joined by that gentleman.

"Aren't you hungry, old chap?" asked Gerald, as he came into the garden.

"Rather," retorted Ronald; "I was wondering when you were going to turn up."

"Hungry!" said Foster, raising his eyes, "and he says he's in love—oh, Cupid! what a worshipper you've got!"

Ronald laughed, and put his hand on Foster's shoulder.

"My dear lad," he said, quietly, "love is the least of my troubles. I want to see Carmela free from all this annoyance and then——"

"And then," repeated Foster, as they walked towards the breakfast-room.

"You'll see as true a lover as ever sighed his soul out to a midnight pillow," laughed Ronald; "now come and have some breakfast, I'm starving."

"What time do you think our friend will arrive?" asked Foster, as they sat down to the table.

"Oh, about three, I should imagine," said Ronald, attacking a fried sole, with a good appetite. "I wonder what the deuce she wants to see me about?"

"Humph! that's a puzzler," said the barrister, lightly; "but I don't think I'm far wrong when I say it will be all about Vassalla."

Ronald laughed, and went on with his breakfast. He was singularly light-hearted, this young man, because an idea had entered his mind that all would yet be well. If it were not for hope and sanguine expectations, where would our pleasure in the future be?

They finished their breakfast, and then went out for a walk; saw the house where Shelley lived, on which is a tablet, erected by Sir William Clayton, and interviewed the landlady of the hotel into which a portion of the place is turned.

"Don't remember 'im," said the landlady, when they asked about the poet; "I think he was afore my time."

"And this is fame!" ejaculated Foster, when they left. "Shelley isn't even remembered by name;" and he began to spout Horace, when Ronald stopped him.

"Don't be classical, old chap; but look at these old parties."

The old parties consisted of two old women, who informed the gentlemen that they were each eighty years old, and had never been out of the town. So Ronald gave them each a shilling, and walked away with his friend.

"I daresay they are much happier than we are," he said, sighing.

"Better to be a butterfly, and enjoy life for a day, than a tortoise, and sleep out a hundred years," said Foster, sapiently; "depend upon it, life is made up of quality, not quantity."

They strolled down to Marlow Church, and then to that tumble-down heap of cottages immortalized by Fred. Walker, the picturesque aspect of which struck Ronald very strongly.

"I don't know much about pictures," said the Australian, frankly, "and I haven't the eye of an artist, but I do admire these mellow-tinted roofs, so different from the galvanized tin of the colonies."

Then they went across the bridge, saw the river full of boats with their light-hearted occupants, had a drink at the Anglers Hotel, and looked out over the foaming waters of the Weir, murmuring like the humming of bees, and ultimately went back to the Crown Hotel, up the long street, with the old little shops on either side.

After they had some luncheon, consisting of bread and cheese and beer, they sat in the dining-room in a kind of somnolent state, smoking steadily, until a waiter came, and said that a lady had called to see them.

"Why, what's the time?" asked Ronald, sleepily, tumbling to his feet.

"Three o'clock, sir," returned the waiter.

"The Devil!" ejaculated Ronald. "I say, old boy, here's Mrs. Verschoyle."

"Right you are," answered Foster, awake and alert at once; "I'm coming—where is the lady?"

"In the sitting-room upstairs, sir," replied the waiter.

They went upstairs to the sitting-room, and found a lady, closely veiled, waiting for them. She arose when they entered, and looked from one to the other in a doubtful way.

"Mr. Monteith?" she asked.

"I have the honour to bear that name," replied Ronald, stepping forward. "You are Mrs. Verschoyle?"

The lady bowed and threw back her veil, disclosing a countenance so like Carmela's, that Ronald was startled for a moment.

"You will wonder what I've come about," said Mrs. Verschoyle, resuming her seat; "so I may as well tell you at once—it is to stop my sister's marriage with the Marchese Vassalla."

Gerald glanced at Ronald, and as their eyes met the same thought was in their minds.

"Jealousy!"

"But why do you come to us?" said Ronald, politely; "we cannot stop the marriage."

How he fervently wished he could!

"Yes, you can," she replied, quietly; "you are looking for the murderer of my husband."

Both the young men stared; what was she going to say?

"My sister and I are not very good friends," said Mrs. Verschoyle; "but I don't want to see her married to a man guilty of a crime."

"Guilty of a crime!" cried Ronald, springing to his feet; "you don't mean to say that Vassalla——"

"Is the murderer of Leopold Verschoyle," she said. "Yes, I swear it."

Ronald sat down again, and looked helplessly at Foster, who came to his aid.

"This is a very serious charge you make, madam," said Foster, gravely; "are you sure?"

She sprang to her feet in a fury.

"Sure!" she hissed, viciously; "of course I am sure; you have been looking for the murderer of my husband, and I tell you the man, then you doubt my word—bah!"

Foster was quite unmoved by her violence.

"I always presume a man's innocent till he is proved guilty," he said, quietly; "so that must be my excuse; but are you sure Vassalla committed this crime?"

"I will tell you all about it," said Mrs. Verschoyle, sitting down again; "when I married Mr. Verschoyle, my cousin Matteo was in love with me."

"So your sister said," interposed Ronald, gravely.

140

"He swore he would kill Leopold Verschoyle if he got the chance, and he has kept his word. I was on board and saw him."

"Saw him commit the crime!"

"Not so much as that," she replied; "but I will explain. I met my husband in Valletta, and went on board to see him."

"You denied doing so in your letter to Vassalla," said Foster.

"Ah! he showed you that—it was to save him I wrote it. I am the only witness who could prove him guilty, and I said I was not on board, so in the case of his being found out, I would not have to appear against him."

"How was the crime committed?" asked Ronald.

"I saw my husband on board, but did not speak to him. I heard him mention the number of his cabin to you, and then leave. Matteo Vassalla, who was beside me, followed him."

"And you?"

"I remained where I was, but I did not think Matteo was going to commit a crime, or I would have gone with him."

"When did you see Vassalla again?"

"I went to my husband's cabin, and met Vassalla coming out. He tried to prevent me from going in, but I entered, and saw my husband dead, with Matteo's stiletto in his breast. Matteo implored me to be silent, and I obeyed. I went on shore at once, and wrote the letter you saw. I would have kept silent still, only I heard that he was going to marry my sister, and determined to save her."

"You say Vassalla's stiletto was in poor Verschoyle's breast," said Foster quietly, fixing his keen eyes on her face. "Will you kindly describe the weapon?"

"An ordinary stiletto," she replied, "with a curiously carved ivory handle, representing the head of Bacchus surrounded with wreaths of grapes and vine leaves."

"Yes, that is the description of the weapon," said Foster; "but how do you know it was Vassalla's?"

"Because my sister told me she had given it to him."

Ronald started, and would have spoken, as he remembered Carmela had said the same thing; but Foster stopped him.

"You say," observed the barrister, smoothly, "that Miss Cotoner gave your cousin the stiletto; may I ask when?"

"Oh, six or seven years ago."

"And it has been in Vassalla's possession ever since?"

"Yes," defiantly; "who else could have it?"

Foster made no answer, so Ronald took up the conversation.

"What motive had Vassalla for committing this crime?" he asked, in a puzzled tone; "he would not have nourished revenge all these years."

"Ah, you don't know a Maltese gentleman," said Mrs. Verschoyle; "he never forgets an insult. My husband insulted him seven years ago, and he swore he would kill him. It is like the Corsican Vendetta with us."

"Are you prepared to make this statement in a court of law?" asked Foster, eyeing her keenly.

"Yes! I will swear to it on the cross."

"Vassalla will have to be arrested."

"Of course," she retorted, defiantly. "I want him to be arrested."

"For the murder of your husband at Valletta?"

"Yes!"

"Good! We will go up to London to-night, and take out a warrant."

"The sooner the better!" she said, vindictively.

"Will you let me offer you some refreshment?" said Ronald, as he arose to leave the room.

"Yes; send me a glass of brandy and soda," she replied. "I feel worn out."

Ronald bowed, and then went out with Foster to see after their things. They sent up the drink to Mrs. Verschoyle, and then Ronald wrote a letter to Carmela, telling her he was going up to London on business, but did not mention what. Foster paid the bill, got their dressing-bags, and in a few minutes they were on their way to the station.

While Foster was getting the tickets, Mrs. Verschoyle being on the platform, Ronald took the opportunity to ask his friend a question.

"Do you think her story is true?" he asked.

"If it isn't, Vassalla can easily clear himself." was the ambiguous reply.

CHAPTER XXV

GUILTY OR NOT GUILTY

Meanwhile Vassalla, quite unconscious of the storm that was about to break over his head, was enjoying himself in London, and had made arrangements to go to Marlow and see Carmela. He thought he had quite subdued Mrs. Verschoyle, and that every impediment to his marriage was removed. So he sat in his room at the Langham, smoking a cigar and moralizing complacently on the state of affairs.

"Fortune favours me," he said, aloud, idly watching the blue wreaths of smoke curling round his head. "I have silenced that devilish Bianca, and won my beautiful Carmela—both at the same time. But, how wonderful it is that the death of Verschoyle should have been the means of winning me both a wife and a fortune Now, when I am married, I must be quiet. I will take my charming wife to Malta, and live on the estate. She does not care for me now; but she will grow fond—yes—she will grow fond."

And so he went on building castles in the air, and dreaming vain dreams, that were destined never to become true, for at that moment there came a knock at the door, which, if he had known its full purport, would have alarmed him as much as the knocking at the gate did Macbeth. But, as he did not know, he merely called out, "Come in," and went on smoking.

Enter a puzzled-looking waiter, showing in Mrs. Verschoyle, Ronald Monteith, Gerald Foster, and a stranger. Vassalla, turning his head, saw them, and sprang to his feet in astonishment.

"What the devil—" he began, but Mrs. Verschoyle interrupted him.

"That is the Marchese Vassalla," she said, pointing to the dumbfoundered Maltese gentleman; whereat the stranger advanced and produced a warrant.

"Matteo Vassalla, I arrest you in the Queen's name——"

"Arrest me!" interrupted the Marchese.

"For the murder of Leopold Verschoyle," finished the detective.

"Is this a joke?" asked Vassalla, angrily.

"You will not find it so," said Ronald.

"It is my duty to inform you," said the detective, stolidly, "that whatever you say will be used in evidence at your trial."

"Bah!" snarled Vassalla, with a gesture of contempt, turning his back on the officer of the law. "Who accuses me of this crime?"

"I do," said Mrs. Verschoyle, stepping forward.

"You!" he cried out, recoiling; "you are mad to do such a thing."

"No, I am not mad," retorted Mrs. Verschoyle, "but I would have been if I had let you marry Carmela."

"Oh!" he said, viciously, looking at Ronald; "so this is a plot to rob me of my promised wife."

"She is not your promised wife," cried Ronald, boldly; "she made the promise under compulsion—now she is free."

"To marry you," said Vassalla, savagely.

"If she'll have me—yes," retorted Monteith.

The Marchese turned to Foster.

"Mr.—whatever your name is," he said, "do you believe this charge?"

"Mrs. Verschoyle says you committed the murder;" returned Foster.

"Mrs. Verschoyle," said Matteo, contemptuously, "is a madwoman."

"Am I?" she returned quietly; "you'll find there's some method in my madness."

"I can disprove the whole charge," said Vassalla, moving towards his writing-table.

"Come, sir," said the detective, "we must be going."

"Going——with you?" retorted Vassalla, in an angry tone, "are you mad? I can disprove this charge," and he threw open the desk and took his portfolio from it.

"Try," said Mrs. Verschoyle, laconically.

Muttering a curse, the Marchese opened his portfolio, and ran through a number of letters. Suddenly he turned round with a ghastly face:

"Where is the paper?" he asked.

"What paper?" said Mrs. Verschoyle, calmly.

"What paper? Curse you!" he cried; "you know the paper I mean—the one written by your husband, whom you accuse me of killing."

"I know of no paper," she said, quietly, with a sneer; "this is a fabrication to delay justice.

"I tell you it's false," cried Vassalla, in despair; "I did not kill the man. I defy you to press this charge. When the time comes I can prove my innocence, and I decline to make any statement now."

"Prove your innocence," she said, sarcastically, "with the missing paper, I suppose?"

"Yes; and you know where it is," he said.

"Maltese dog," she shrieked, "you lie," and she would have sprung forward, only Ronald her back.

"I have to thank you for this," said Vassalla to Ronald, as he put on his hat and coat, "but, I do not forget, I will repay you; and as for you, jade that you are, I'll prove myself innocent and then punish you."

"Bah! I defy you," she said, contemptuously; "you'll never marry Carmela, but hang—hang, like the dog you are!"

"Confound it, Mrs. Verschoyle, leave the man alone," said Ronald, rather annoyed at the way she was behaving.

Vassalla walked to the door with the detective beside him, and faced round as he was going out.

"As sure as there's a God in heaven," he said, proudly, "I am innocent, and that woman only brings this accusation against me to satisfy her absurd jealousy. I can prove my innocence, and she"—pointing to Mrs. Verschoyle—"holds the proof."

When the door closed, Foster turned to Mrs. Verschoyle.

"What does he mean?" asked the lawyer.

"I don't know," she said. "I possess no proof of his innocence, and I'm ready to go into the witness box, and swear he killed my husband."

"He says he is not guilty," said Ronald.

"He'll say anything to save his neck, but he is guilty; I'll see him hanged, till he is dead."

There was something so repulsive in the vindictiveness of this woman, that both the young men were disgusted, and left the room followed by Mrs. Verschoyle, who was laughing to herself in a satisfied manner.

"Why don't you thank me?" she said, savagely, to Ronald; "I have prevented Carmela from marrying another man, and secured your happiness."

"I don't care for happiness that is founded on the ruin of another man," said Monteith, coldly.

"Bah! you are a fool; he is guilty."

"That," said Foster, quietly, "has yet to be proved."

She flashed a look of anger at him, then went out of the hotel door, and stepped into a hansom.

"I will see you to-morrow," she called out, "and then I can prove that what I say is true."

The cab drove off, leaving Foster and Ronald looking at one another.

"What do you think?" asked the Australian.

"I don't know what to think," said Foster: "the Marchese says he is innocent."

145

"All men accused of a crime say that."

"Yes; but I fancy in this case it's true."

"Then, who killed Verschoyle?"

"I believe his wife did."

"What!"

"Yes; I think she's accusing Vassalla out of jealousy."

"But he did not accuse her of the crime."

"No, he certainly did not," said Foster, musingly. "It's a queer case. What was the paper he was talking about?"

"I don't know," said Ronald. "It is, as you say, a very queer case. I'm going down to Marlow to-morrow."

"What for?"

"I want to see Carmela, and tell her all about the affair."

"Yes, it will be best for you to do that," said Foster. "Perhaps she may throw some light on the affair."

"I don't think so; we know everything she knows."

"I expect the real reason you want to go down is, to tell her she is free?" said Foster, quizzically.

"She's not free yet," retorted Ronald.

"To all intents and purposes she is."

"I want to hear from her own lips that she considers herself free."

"But you don't think she'll marry Vassalla now—a man accused of murder?"

"I don't know," said Ronald, with a sigh, "women are such queer creatures. She may consider herself doubly bound, now he's down on his luck."

"I'll bet you she don't!"

"I'll bet you she does!"

"Very well," said Foster, philosophically, "the wager will be decided to-morrow night."

146

CHAPTER XXVI

CARMELA SAYS "YES"

Meanwhile, quite unaware of the troubles in which Vassalla was involved, Carmela was enjoying herself very much at Bellfield. She was in much better spirits than she had been previously, as her conversation with Foster and Ronald had relieved her mind of a great weight, and she had come to the conclusion that her sister was not guilty, in which case she would not have to marry her cousin. Everyone stopping at Bellfield was in excellent spirits, and so Carmela felt the influence of merry company, and was as gay and joyous as anyone present.

It being Bell's birthday, they decided to celebrate it with a picnic at Medmenham Abbey, and were all down at Hurley Lock, embarking in the boats. Pat was especially exuberant, as he had discovered, beyond all doubt, that Miss Lester was in love with him, and he was only waiting for a good opportunity to propose. A merrier party were never on the river than the young people from Hurley.

And what a delightful morning it was on the river in this glowing July weather. They had no servants with them, as Sir Mark preferred full freedom for once, and the young men rowed the boats quickly up, passing other gay parties on the way.

Up the placid stream they went, past Lady Place, with its quaint old roof and mellow-tinted walls, under the arched wooden bridge that springs over the Thames; up through the still waters with the broad green meadows on each side, filled with quiet cattle, until the gables of the Ferry Hotel at Medmenham came in sight, and here they went on shore. They found the lawn crowded with young men in flannels, and young ladies in boating costumes; went to the ruins of the old Abbey, with all its memories of the Hell-fire Club, and the orgies they held therein.

It is said that the present Abbey is a pinchbeck affair, and the only genuine ruins of the old Abbey are to be found in the solitary pillar which stands at the back, near the haystacks; but surely the great building, with its ruined tower, overgrown with ivy; its quaint windows, scribbled all over with names, and its low-roofed door, with the famous motto, "Fay ce que voudrais," are genuine enough.

After they had explored the Abbey, all the party strolled away inland to see the lions of the locality. An old-fashioned street it is

147

that leads through the village of Medmenham, with the flint-built houses on either side, overgrown with ivy, and one can imagine a cavalier, after the defeat of unlucky Charles Stuart, spurring swiftly down the lonely road, in his wild flight for safety.

Then the church, with the square Norman tower, around which the rooks are always wheeling and cawing, casting its mighty shadow over the green grass, beneath which the quiet dead sleep soundly, as they have done for so many hundred years. Opposite the church stands the "Dog and Badger," a very old hostel, with mellow-tinted roofs and numerous gables, and within, low-ceilinged rooms with great beams overhead, and queer, twisted staircases and unexpected cupboards all over the house.

At the back, high up on the hill, and commanding a magnificent view of the Thames Valley, stands the stern-looking old farm-house, said to have been mentioned in the Domesday Book, and where Charles II. and pretty, witty Nell Gwynne are reported to have stayed for a night. Then, farther on, the quiet little village of Hambledon, through which it is said Charles I. rode with a brilliant train of gallant cavaliers, on his way to meet his rebellious subjects. The whole neighbourhood is full of antiquities and traditions, which lend a peculiar charm to the place.

When they grew weary of sight-seeing, the whole party went down again to the river, and getting into the boats, rowed up the stream for a considerable distance, and ultimately decided to hold their picnic just below Hambledon Lock, with the pleasant murmur of the Weir in their ears.

Such a scene of confusion, getting out the luncheon—everyone seated round in attitudes graceful and otherwise, with the clatter of dishes, the popping of champagne corks, and a perfect Babel of voices.

"This is jolly," said Pat, with his mouth full. "I'm fond of Arcadian simplicity."

"Especially when it's accompanied by champagne," cried Bubbles, raising his glass to his lips.

"Begad, you're not slow in finding out what I mean," said Ryan, laughing, and filling his glass.

"Imitation's the sincerest flattery," observed Miss Lester, gaily, trying to cut up a rather wiry chicken. "I believe this fowl was a pedestrian, his legs are so tough."

"Try some of the breast," said Sir Mark; "at all events, it hasn't got eight legs, like the birds you get on board ship."

"That's true enough," cried Pat; "everyone seems to get legs of fowls on board—perhaps they're like Manx men,—got three legs."

"Or a hundred, like a centipede," said Bubbles.

148

"Oh, this conversation is frivolous," said Pat, raising his glass, "so I'll propose a toast: to the health of Miss Trevor, and many happy returns of the day."

This was, of course, drank by everyone with acclamation, and then the male portion of the company sang, "She's a jolly good fellow," rather incongruously, it must be confessed.

"I wish Monteith were here," said Pat, when this was done.

Carmela said nothing, but looked much, for in her secret heart, that is just what she had been wishing. At this moment they heard a wild whoop from the river, and saw a boat coming quickly up the stream, rowed by a single man.

"Gad," cried Bubbles, who had the sharpest eyes of anyone; "it's Monteith himself. Speak of the Devil——"

"Hold your tongue," said Pat, "don't be personal."

It was Ronald, looking happy and jolly in his flannels, quite a different being from the gloomy youth of the previous week. He soon brought his light little craft to shore, and sprang on to the green turf, to be welcomed.

"My dear lad," said Sir Mark, "I am delighted to see you, especially as your arrival is so unexpected."

"How did you find us out?" asked Carmela, giving him her hand.

"Oh, easily enough," replied Ronald, gaily. "I came down to Maidenhead, drove over to Bellfield, and finding it was deserted, learnt from the servants where you were, so here I am."

"Hurrah for that," cried Pat; "is drink a curse?"

"Egad, I'm not sure. I'll try, if you've no objection," said Ronald.

Whereat, Mr. Ryan grinned, and handed his friend a glass and a bottle, all to himself.

The luncheon was resumed, and then the party began to break up into little groups. Pat, of course, going with Miss Lester, while Bell went under the wing of Bubbles, though she secretly sighed for the society of Gerald Foster. So, in a short time, Ronald found himself alone with Carmela, whose eyes turned on him with eager expectation.

"Well," she asked, "is there anything new?"

"Yes; I've seen your sister."

"And she is innocent?"

"Yes, and moreover, has told us who committed the crime."

Carmela was startled.

"Does she know who did it?"

"She says so. Your cousin!"

"What, Matteo!" rising to her feet. "Oh, impossible!"

149

"Of course that's what he says, also," said Ronald, shrugging his shoulders; "but your sister accused him and he has been arrested."

"Will they hang him?"

"If they prove him guilty, no doubt; but first, they must prove the case."

"I cannot believe it of my cousin, he had no motive."

"Mrs. Verschoyle says he had—that he was in love with her."

"Yes, he was, seven years ago," said Carmela, not without a certain feminine spite, "but that would not have induced him to kill poor Leopold Verschoyle now. Maltese gentlemen don't avenge themselves in such a cowardly way."

"Well, Vassalla says he can prove his innocence, but there's one thing to be said, the whole secret of Verschoyle's death lies between your sister and Vassalla."

"How on earth will it all end?" said Carmela, in a bewildered tone; "but," with a sudden thought, "if Vassalla is guilty I am not bound to marry him now."

"Of course not," said Ronald, taking one of her hands, "I want you to marry me."

She snatched her hand away.

"How can you talk so at such a time?" she cried, her face flushing.

"Because I love you," he replied, "and I want to have the assurance from your lips that you love me."

"How can you marry the cousin of a possible criminal?"

"I don't care a bit about that: I want to marry you."

"Wait till this affair is ended."

"Oh, I don't mind that; Vassalla will be brought to his trial in a few weeks, and then it will be decided one way or another. But, Carmela," taking her hand once more, "when it is all over will you marry me?"

She paused a moment, then said simply—

"Yes."

Ronald took her in his arms and kissed her.

150

CHAPTER XXVII

EXIT MRS. VERSCHOYLE

Of course it is not to be wondered at that the arrest of Vassalla made a great sensation. True Vassalla was not a very well known man; but then the strangeness of the case, which was reported with numerous embellishments in all the papers, attracted everybody's notice. And then the way the crime had been brought home to him by the divorced wife of the dead man—in fact, it was quite a romance.

The curious part of the whole case was that Vassalla obstinately refused to say anything in his own defence, and his persistent silence was taken as an acknowledgment of his guilt. But the Marchese only smiled grimly when spoken to, and said he could defend himself well enough when the time came, and, moreover, would be in a position to punish Mrs. Verschoyle.

As for that lady, she was quite the heroine of the hour—not exactly in a complimentary sense, perhaps—but everybody wanted to see a woman with such an exciting history, who had divorced her husband, and then accused her cousin of being his murderer. Plenty of papers wanted to interview her, but she declined to allow herself to be seen, and generally sat at home in a quiet, private hotel off the Strand, where she exulted over the downfall of Vassalla.

"He wouldn't marry me," she said to herself, vindictively; "well, we'll see how he likes being in prison for murder."

Carmela came up to town, and had an interview with her, in which Mrs. Verschoyle lost her temper, as usual.

"He wanted to marry you—he wanted to marry you," she hissed repeatedly.

"I couldn't help that," retorted Carmela, angrily; "I certainly did not want to marry him, and would never have become engaged to him if it had not been to save you."

"Ha! ha! to save me from the gallows, I suppose—bah. I do not believe it? he would have accused me of the murder of my husband, the Maltese dog; but he shall die for it—yes, he shall die."

"Are you sure he committed this—this crime?" said Carmela, hesitatingly.

"Yes, I am sure. Did I not meet him coming out of the cabin on that night; was the stiletto in the dead man's breast not the one you gave him years ago? am I sure—bah! if he is innocent, let him prove it."

There was nothing to be got out of Mrs. Verschoyle, who was simply mad with anger, and grew purple in the face, till Carmela thought she would break a blood-vessel.

"You ought to be grateful to me," she said, furiously; "but for me you would have married Vassalla, and then what of your Australian lover?"

"You can leave my Australian lover out of the question," said Carmela, with great spirit. "I am only waiting for this unhappy affair to be settled, in order to marry him."

"Yes, do, do," cried Mrs. Verschoyle; "and go with him to Australia. Put the ocean between us. I never wish to see your face again. If it had not been for you, my husband would have loved me."

"He did love you," said Carmela, "but your temper drove him away."

At this Mrs. Verschoyle burst out into a storm of anger; so, in order to put a stop to the scene, Carmela left the room, and went back to the Langham, where Sir Mark Trevor waited her.

"I don't want to see my sister again," she said, firmly, and she never did.

Of course, when the trial came on, the court was crowded with the most noted people in London, anxious to see the end of this strange case. It ended more dramatically than they thought it would.

Vassalla entered the dock in a calm, cool manner, and glanced quickly round the court, of course everyone thinking he was a hardened scoundrel for not exhibiting more emotion. He had engaged a famous lawyer to defend him, and this gentleman was smiling quietly to himself, and by no means looking as if he thought the case a grave one. Foster was in the court, together with Ronald and Sir Mark Trevor, all listening eagerly to the introductory address of the prosecuting counsel.

He stated the whole story, which had already appeared in the papers, but with some slight variations:—

That Leopold Verschoyle had been married to Miss Bianca Cotoner seven years before, with whom the prisoner was also very much in love. When she married the deceased, the prisoner had sworn he would kill him. The prisoner, however, did not carry his resolution into effect at that time, but went travelling about Europe, and Miss Cotoner married the deceased. They did not live happily together, and separated, which separation was afterwards followed by a divorce, owing to the deceased's infidelity with another woman called Elsie Macgregor.

The deceased then travelled all over the world, and was coming to England on board the P. and O. steamer "Neptune," which stopped at Malta. While there the deceased went on shore, and was recognised by his wife, who went on board to speak to him, The prisoner was also on board with the sister of the deceased, called Miss Carmela Cotoner, and then—according to Mrs. Verschoyle, who was the principal witness—recognised deceased, and heard him tell Mr. Monteith, another witness, the number of his cabin.

The prisoner then disappeared from Mrs. Verschoyle's side, and when she went to speak to her husband, she met the prisoner coming out of the cabin, and though he tried to prevent her, she looked in and saw her husband—or rather her husband that had been, lying dead with a stiletto in his breast. The stiletto, as will appear from the evidence of Miss Carmela Cotoner, was given by that lady to the prisoner, and was used in the commission of this crime.

With a few concluding remarks, the counsel for the prosecution sat down, and the witnesses were called. During all the discourse the Marchese never moved a muscle, but sat in the dock as still as death.

The first witness called was Ronald, who repeated the story the dead man had told him, and, during his examination, the paper written by Carmela was put in evidence.

He was followed by Carmela, who deposed that she had given the stiletto in question to the prisoner, and also said that the letter produced was written by her, and not by the wife of the deceased, Mrs. Verschoyle.

Q. You were on board when Mrs. Verschoyle came?

A. Yes.

Q. Was she alone?

A. At first, yes. Afterwards she was escorted by the Marchese Vassalla.

Q. Did you see her again?

A. No.

Q. When the Marchese saw you again, what time was it?

A. About a quarter-past nine: just after the boat started.

Q. Did he make any remark?

A. None, except that my sister could not find me in the crowd, and had to go ashore without saying good-bye.

Q. Was he agitated?

A. No; he was in his usual spirits.

This closed Carmela's examination; and the next to go into the witness-box was Mrs. Verschoyle, pale and haggard, but who glanced angrily at the prisoner, as she kissed the book. She repeated the story she had told to Ronald and Foster. That she was with Vassalla, and wanted to see her husband. Both herself and her cousin heard him tell the number of his cabin; and though she tried to get near her husband, she was prevented by the crowd. Afterwards she missed Vassalla, and on going along to see her husband in the cabin, she found Vassalla coming out. He tried to prevent her going in, but she insisted, and found her husband lying dead with a stiletto in his breast.

Q. You know to whom the stiletto belonged?

A. Yes, to the prisoner; it was given to him by my sister.

Q. What did the prisoner say when you met him?

A. He implored me not to tell, and for the sake of the honour of our family I complied.

Q. Do you know by doing so you run the risk of being taken as an accomplice?

A. (Mrs. Verschoyle getting angry). I know nothing of English customs. I am a Maltese lady.

Q. Did you ever hear the prisoner threaten the deceased?

A. Yes, very many times; he wanted to marry me, and when I married the deceased, he swore he would revenge himself.

Q. That was seven years ago; did he do so lately?

A. Many times. (Here Vassalla shrugged his shoulders).

This was the close of Mrs. Verschoyle's examination, and was supposed by the people present to be conclusive evidence of the prisoner's guilt. There was no evidence for the prosecution, and so the counsel for the defence arose to make his speech, a speech which considerably startled everyone.

In the first place, he said Mrs. Verschoyle was guilty of perjury—(sensation)—gross perjury; it was true the prisoner was once in love with her, but that was seven years ago, and he had long since forgotten his passion. The prisoner was on board the "Neptune" on the night in question, going to England, and Mrs. Verschoyle also came on board; she wanted to see her husband, and the prisoner, hearing the number of the cabin, volunteered to look for him; he was considerably delayed in the crowd, and did not reach the cabin for some time, particularly as he met one of the stewards, who asked him about his luggage, and engaged his attention for nearly ten minutes.

When he reached the cabin, he knocked, and, getting no reply, entered. He found the deceased dead (sensation), having committed suicide, and on the washstand by the berth was a letter directed to Mr. R. Monteith, a friend of the deceased, stating that he had committed suicide. This paper the prisoner took charge of, and was coming out with it, when he met Mrs. Verschoyle. He told her what had occurred, and she was so shocked with the news that she went straight on shore.

The prisoner was blameable in not producing the paper at the inquest, but had anyone been accused of the crime, he would have produced it. With regard to the stiletto, it was once the property of the prisoner, but he had given it to the deceased as a parting gift before he left for Australia, for both the deceased and prisoner were good friends then.

The wife of the deceased, Mrs. Verschoyle, knew that the deceased had the dagger in his possession, as the prisoner showed a letter to her from deceased, acknowledging the gift of stiletto (letter produced). She was in love with prisoner, who refused to marry her, being in love with Miss Carmela Cotoner, to whom he was engaged to be married. Mrs. Verschoyle, hearing of this, came here from Valletta, and had a private interview with prisoner. During his absence from his room at the Langham Hotel she stole the confession made by the deceased, and it is now in her possession—she——

"That's a lie!" cried Mrs. Verschoyle, mad with fury, rising from her seat.

"Silence in the court!" cried the usher.

"I will not be silent. It is an infamous lie. That man is guilty of murder. He killed my husband, and by God!—by God!——"

All at once she stopped speaking, her face turned to a ghastly pallor, and appeared convulsively drawn to one side as if by a stroke of paralysis. Every eye in the Court was fastened on that solitary figure, and there was an awful pause of expectancy. Another moment and she fell prone on the floor with a heavy thud.

The Court was in an uproar at the strange occurrence, and at first it was thought she had merely fainted through excitement. A doctor, however, being present, came forward, and knelt down by Mrs. Verschoyle, who was now breathing stertorously.

He glanced at her pain-drawn face, felt her pulse, and while he was doing so the heavy breathing stopped.

"What is the matter?" asked the judge, bending forward; "is it a faint?"

The doctor raised his head.

"No, my Lord—it is death!"

"Death!" echoed several voices, and the Court arose in confusion.

"Yes—she has burst a blood vessel in the brain."

Dead! Dead! Yes, Mrs. Verschoyle was dead—in the very moment of her triumph!

155

CHAPTER XXVIII

A SCRAP OF PAPER

THE sudden death of Mrs. Verschoyle so appalled everyone, that the trial was adjourned. A great sensation was created when the report came out in the papers, and numerous were the theories as to how the trial would end, now the principal witness was dead.

As a matter of fact, according to public opinion, the only thing that could prove the innocence of Vassalla, was the production of the letter written by the dead man, and alleged to have been stolen by Mrs. Verschoyle, and after the body had been removed, Ronald, in company with Foster and Vassalla's lawyer, went to look for it.

"What shall we do if she has destroyed it?" said Ronald, as they walked along.

"Oh, she hasn't destroyed it," replied Vassalla's lawyer, whose name was Winks; "she would have produced it at the eleventh hour."

"Then you think such a paper is in existence?" said Foster.

"I'm certain of it, and Mrs. Verschoyle knew the Marchese was innocent. She only accused him out of jealousy."

"But why did he not deny the charge at once, instead of letting himself be placed in such a perilous position?"

"I don't know," said Winks; "he never gave me any explanation. But he knew he was safe, for even should the paper not be forthcoming, the evidence of the deceased, that Vassalla had given him the dagger, would save him. If he hadn't the stiletto, he couldn't have killed him with it, that's flat."

"But Verschoyle distinctly denied to me that he had any intention of committing suicide," said Ronald.

Winks shrugged his shoulders.

"Changed his mind, I suppose. He evidently did it on the spur of the moment. But here we are, at last."

They went into the hotel, and were shown into the late Mrs. Verschoyle's room by the landlady, who had heard of her lodger's death, and was much scared thereat.

"I knew she'd break a blood-vessel," she said, smoothing her black silk dress; "the rages she got into were awful. They won't bring the corpse here, I hope?"

"No," replied Ronald, "it has been taken to Sir Mark Trevor's town house."

"Didn't know he had one," said Foster; "he stops at the Langham."

"Oh, yes; he dislikes his town house immensely, and being a student of human nature, likes the life of an hotel. I don't think he's far wrong, myself."

They went to Mrs. Verschoyle's room and hunted everywhere for the paper so much required, but in vain. Ransacked her desk, looked through her trunks, but without any satisfactory result.

"Perhaps she's left it about for greater safety," said Foster, referring to Poe's queer story of the "Purloined Letter."

The landlady was called up and questioned, but denied ever seeing the paper.

"Perhaps she had it with her," she suggested, as the three gentlemen looked blankly at one another.

No, the body had been searched, so they left the hotel in despair.

"Looks had for Vassalla," said Ronald.

"Not a bit!" retorted the stout-hearted Winks, "the stiletto evidence will get him off; but Mrs. Verschoyle evidently intended he should swing, and has perhaps destroyed the paper."

He went off, so Ronald invited Foster to dine with him at the "Tavistock," an invitation which that gentleman accepted. All the newsboys along the Strand were calling out sensational sentences about the case, and Ronald bought some papers to read. When they entered the hotel the clerk handed Ronald a letter that had been waiting for him all day. It was addressed in a woman's handwriting, and Monteith opened it carelessly, but on glancing at the contents he gave a shout which startled Foster.

"What's the matter, old chap?"

"The missing paper!" gasped Ronald, holding it out; and so it was. Foster took it and read it.

"My dear Monteith—I'm sick of life, and as I've no one to consult about staying in it, I'm going into the next world, straight off. Lionel Ventin."

"This puts Vassalla's innocence beyond all doubt," said Foster, "but the signature will have to be proved—can you do it?"

"No," replied Monteith; "but there's Mrs. Taunton."

"Yes!—we'll have to see her," said the barrister, putting the letter in his pocket; "but how the deuce did it come to you?"

"I don't know," said Ronald blankly, "unless she never intended Vassalla should suffer, but sent me this to-day and the case would have been squashed to-morrow. I believe she was mad."

Foster thought so also, especially when they went back to the hotel and found how the letter had been posted. Mrs. Verschoyle

157

had placed it in an envelope and directed it to Ronald, but, evidently changing her mind, went out leaving it on the table. A waiter coming in had seen it, so posted it at once thinking it was an oversight on Mrs. Verschoyle's part.

There was no difficulty in proving the document to be authentic, as Mrs. Taunton affirmed at once that both the writing and the signature were in her brother's handwriting, and supported her assertion by producing his letters to her, which put the whole question beyond a doubt.

This curious ending to a curious case made a great sensation, but Vassalla took his acquittal very coolly. He was more annoyed at Carmela's refusal to marry him than anything else, as that young lady not only refused to see him, but wrote a letter and upbraided him for the falsehood he had told, regarding her sister's guilt, to gain her hand.

Vassalla did not answer the letter, but seeing there was no hope for him, went off to America, and found among the passengers the Bishop of Patagonia and his wife, accompanied by Mrs. Pellypop, who had insisted on coming. The Bishop yielded, in the secret hope that some benevolent cannibal might eat the old lady, but she evidently did not look inviting enough, as she is still alive and hearty.

Mrs. Verschoyle, whose unhappy fate no one particularly deplored, was buried in Kensal Green Cemetery, and lies there at rest, with all her loves, her hates, and ambitions. Carmela could not honestly pretend to mourn, but she regretted that the last interview she had with her was such a stormy one.

Ronald went down again to Hurley, and spent the summer months on the river in the delightful company of Carmela, who, now that the cloud, so long overshadowing her life, had passed away, was perfectly happy. They were wrapped up in one another, and paid no attention to the other guests at Bellfield.

This was decidedly selfish, and would have been resented, only it so happened that two other couples under Sir Mark Trevor's hospitable roof were doing precisely the same thing.

In the first place, Mr. Patrick Ryan had persuaded Kate Lester to agree to change her name for his own.

"A fair exchange is no robbery," observed Pat when he proposed. "I give you my name and you give me yourself."

"And you call that a fair exchange," retorted his lady-love. "I think you're getting the best of the bargain—I'm marrying a poor man."

"Of course," said Pat cheerfully, "that's where my self-sacrifice comes in. I can't support myself, so I'm going to support you—we can live on bread-and-cheese and——

"Well?"

"If you've no objection, we'll have an acting charade on the last word."

They did!

Sir Mark was resigned to the infliction of two loving couples staying with him, but he did feel rather crushed when Gerald Foster asked him to bestow Bell's hand upon him.

"Good gracious!" ejaculated the astonished baronet, "it's a catching disease—I'm glad Mrs. Pellypop isn't here, or I'd fall a victim to matrimony myself."

He liked Foster, however, and moreover saw he was a man likely to make his mark in the world, so agreed to the engagement, and resigned himself, in a Christian spirit, to the awful fact of living in the same house with three young men engaged to the same number of young women.

"I feel like an elderly Cupid," he said plaintively; "the only remedy for this epidemic of love-making is to get them married as soon as possible."

So as soon as possible the marriages took place all at the same time in the church at Marlow, and the excitement was great over the treble event, as such a thing had not occurred in the neighbourhood within the memory of man.

It will be interesting news to all matrimonial pessimists that none of these marriages have as yet turned out failures, or does there seem the least chance of any such possibility.

Foster, with the assistance of his father-in-law, soon got plenty of briefs, and is now a brilliant Q.C., cherishing dreams of the Bench and the Woolsack.

Miss Lester's uncle dying, left her all his money, which Pat devoted to restoring the home of his ancestors, where he lives now with his pretty wife, and is not much troubled, except by his tenants, who won't pay any rent.

And Ronald?

Oh, Ronald is in far-off Australia, and by his side stands the Girl from Malta.

FINIS

9 798889 424857